MIDDLE SCHOOL

JUST MY ROTTEN LUCK

JAMES PATTERSON is the internationally bestselling author of the highly praised Middle School books, *Katt vs. Dogg*, Ali Cross and the I Funny, Jacky Ha-Ha, Treasure Hunters, Dog Diaries and Max Einstein series. James Patterson has been the most borrowed author in UK libraries for the past thirteen years in a row and his books have sold more than 400 million copies worldwide, making him one of the biggest-selling authors of all time. He lives in Florida.

MIDDLE SCHOOL
JUST MY ROTTEN LUCK

JAMES PATTERSON

AND CHRIS TEBBETTS

ILLUSTRATED BY LAURA PARK

9 10

Young Arrow
20 Vauxhall Bridge Road
London SW1V 2SA

Young Arrow is part of the Penguin Random House group of companies
whose addresses can be found at global.penguinrandomhouse.com

First published by Young Arrow in 2015
First published in paperback by Young Arrow in 2016

www.penguin.co.uk

A CIP catalogue record for this book is
available from the British Library

Printed and bound in Great Britain by Clays Ltd, Elcograf S.p.A.

The authorised representative in the EEA is Penguin Random House Ireland,
Morrison Chambers, 32 Nassau Street, Dublin D02 YH68

Penguin Random House is committed to a sustainable future for our
business, our readers and our planet. This book is made from Forest
Stewardship Council® certified paper.

TO MY FAVORITE FOOTBALL FAN,
ILSE TEBBETTS
—C.T.

THIS IS NOT A DRILL

E ver since I've known you—how long has it been now?—I've been getting my butt kicked in about a hundred different ways. Well, the butt-kicking officially stops here.

On this page.

Before the next period

•

That's why this could be my best story yet. I've got a ton of stuff to tell you about. More than ever, in fact. For a while, I thought maybe I'd call this book *The Butt-Kick Stops Here*. Or maybe *Look at Me, I'm Special*. Or *First Kiss*. Or *Rafe Khatchadorian: Secret Agent Artist*.

But I didn't call it any of those things. In case you haven't already noticed, I called this one *Just My Rotten Luck*.

And even though that doesn't sound like the happy-go-luckiest title you've ever heard of (with plenty of good reason), there's a lot that happens in this book that's pretty awesome.

Like me being a football hero.

Yeah, yeah. I know *football* and *Rafe Khatchadorian* don't exactly go together like ham and eggs. But that really was me, hitting the field for the Hills Village Middle School Falcons. It really did happen.

Really, really.

Don't get me wrong. I'm not saying this story is going to be all about touchdowns and cheerleaders screaming my name. (*Obviously*. I mean, have you seen what I look like?)

I'm just saying...well, you know what? Maybe I should start at the beginning. And for that to happen, we have to go back in time a little bit. And *that* means I'm going to need a good old-fashioned flashback. Then a flash-forward, and then who knows what else after that.

So buckle up, people. It's going to be a bumpy ride. All set? Good.

Here comes the flashback!

CHAPTER 2

ROUGH START

Welcome to THE PAST! Don't worry, we didn't go that far. Just three weeks earlier, to be exact.

I was at the tail end of a pretty lousy summer, which is *supposed* to be the best time of the year for most kids. Me, not so much. Camp Wannamorra had been a disaster, and my time at The Program in the Rocky Mountains just about killed me in six different ways. (Well, okay, just *one* way, but still…)

None of that was the worst part, though. That happened on the Friday before school started, when Mom took me to Hills Village Middle School. We had a meeting scheduled with Mrs. Stricker and Mrs. Stonecase so I could get re-enrolled there.

You remember Mrs. Stricker, right? And Mrs. Stonecase too? They're the principal and vice principal of HVMS. They're also sisters—for real. That's like getting twice the trouble for half the price. Not to mention, if there was a Worldwide Khatchadorian Haters Club, they'd be the president and vice president.

So anyway, as soon as I was stuck inside that lion's den (I mean, sitting down in Mrs. Stricker's office), I got a two-ton piece of bad news dropped on my head.

"If Rafe wishes to come back to Hills Village Middle School this fall," Mrs. Stricker said to my mom, "he'll have to be enrolled as a special needs student."

And I was like, "Say WHAT?"

But Stricker wasn't done. She kept going, like a tidal wave of meanness that just couldn't be stopped. "Whether he'll finish middle school on time or have to put in an extra semester or two—or *more*—well, we just can't say at this point," she told us.

And then I was like, "Say WHAAAAAAT???"

I don't know what they call it at your school. IEP. SPED. Special Education. Barnum & Bailey's Three-Ring Circus. At HVMS, the kids have plenty of names for it—just not ones they say when any teachers are around.

And now I was in it.

I tried to talk Stricker, Stonecase, and even Mom out of making this horrible mistake, but they wouldn't budge. Mom wasn't being mean about it or anything. I know she wants what's best for me. She just said I should give it a try.

"We'll see how things go once the school year starts," she said. "Who knows, maybe you'll even like it."

Which is such a MOM thing to say.

In the meantime, if you're thinking this story is all about bad news, don't worry. Some cool stuff happens too, like that first kiss, and some other things I haven't even told you about yet.

But so far? My school year was off to the worst start ever.

And it hadn't even started yet.

CHAPTER 3

SPECIAL

Christmas is special.

Finding a dollar on the ground is special.

Personal pan pizzas with double pepperoni are special.

But getting put in a "special needs" program with "special" classes and no guarantee of getting through middle school anytime *especial*ly soon?

Not so special.

Before we left school that day, Mom and I had a meeting with my new "Learning Skills" teacher, Mr. Edward Fanucci. It's pronounced fuh-noochy, and sounds to me like something you'd eat with tomato sauce.

"Rafe, welcome back to HVMS," he said. "I'm glad we'll be working together this year. And it's Jules, is that right, Mrs. Khatchadorian?"

"Jules is fine," Mom said.

Mr. Fanucci recognized Mom from the diner where she works—Swifty's over on Montgomery Boulevard. She even remembered that he liked his cheeseburgers well done and sat by himself at the counter for breakfast every Sunday morning.

In fact, the two of them were having a great old time talking about cheeseburgers while I sat there thinking about how miserable my life was about to get.

What did all this mean, exactly? Was I just plain dumb? Could I have gotten out of it if I'd paid more attention in school? If I'd eaten more veggies when my mom told me to? If I didn't have an imaginary friend who I used to talk to all the time?

If I wasn't so *weird*?

"Okay, Rafe," Mr. Fanucci finally said, "we need to review your IEP. Then I'll let you go, and you can start enjoying the last few days of your summer vacation."

I wanted to ask how he thought I could *enjoy* anything with this hanging over my head, but I didn't say a word. I just thought, *NONONONO NONONONO!*

Supposedly, *IEP* stands for *Individualized Education Program*. But if you ask me, it was more like *In Extreme Pain*.

I guess Mr. Fanucci could tell I was about as excited as a kid in the dentist's chair, because he started getting all buddy-buddy with me.

"Believe it or not, you're going to be glad for this program," he said. "It's going to help you do better than ever in school, like getting some extra gas in the tank. You'll take most of your classes with everyone else and work with me on your assignments. Three times a week, we'll have our Learning Skills group, with some kids like you who need extra help."

"Kids like me?" I said.

"Yeah," he said. "Kids who learn differently."

Which was just another way of saying SPECIALS. Dummies. Rejects. Weirdos. Freaks.

You know—kids like me.

AMBUSH

You know how I said that day was the worst part of my whole summer? Well, hold on, because the day wasn't over yet.

While Mom was talking to Mr. Fanucci some more, I asked if I could wait out in the parking lot. The last thing I wanted was for anyone to see me hanging around the office and start asking questions.

So there I was, sitting on the bumper of our car and wondering what kind of job a middle school dropout could get (answer: NONE), when my day got a little worse. And by "a little worse," I mean a *lot* worse.

"Yo! Khatcha*DORK*ian!" said a familiar voice.

I looked up and saw...wait for it...or maybe you can guess?

That's right. Miller the Killer.

Yup. Just my rotten luck.

He was coming my way, along with a bunch of guys from the HVMS flag football team. I guess they'd already started practice for the season, because they were all wearing their cleats and headed for the fields behind the school.

Which put me right in their path—like a rickety little straw hut in a hurricane.

When I first went to HVMS, Miller made my life about as enjoyable as a box of rabbit poo that you thought was juicy raisins. The last time we'd tangled, both of us ended up bloody. Mostly because he got my blood all over him.

So you could say we didn't exactly part ways as friends.

"What are *you* doing here?" Miller said. "Don't tell me you're coming back to HVMS."

"Okay," I said. "I won't tell you that."

"Wait," he said, and got that familiar, confused look on his face. "So you *are* coming back?" Miller isn't "special" like me, but he's not exactly the brightest bulb on the Christmas tree either.

"This is going to be good," Jeremy Savin said, and gave Bobby Davidson a fist bump. The way they were all looking at me, it was starting to feel like feeding time in the gorilla house at the zoo.

If I could have, I would have gotten out of there. But what was I going to do, snap my fingers and disappear? Tell him I had to go to the bathroom? (Actually, I *did* have to go to the bathroom, but that wasn't much help.)

And I couldn't tell Miller to shove it either. That would have been like sticking a piece of dynamite in my mouth and handing him a lit match.

Except then I got a lucky break. Coach Shumsky showed up at the top of the football bleachers and started yelling our way.

"Miller! Savin! Davidson!" he said. "You joining us for practice today? Or are you planning on sitting out the opening game this season?"

"Coming, Coach!" Jeremy called.

"Right away, Coach!" Miller said, like they were in the army or something. Trust me when I tell you, these guys take their flag football verrrrrry seriously. Once they get into high school, they'll play full tackle ball. In the meantime, they like to practice their tackling skills on guys like me.

"This isn't over," Miller told me, and pointed a finger right in my face. I could even smell what he'd had for lunch: bologna sandwich, spicy mustard, and grape soda.

"*What's* not over?" I said. "There's nothing… started."

That's when he gave me one of his Miller-sized chest thumps. If I hadn't been shoved up against Mom's bumper, I probably would have fallen flat on my butt. And it wouldn't have been the first time.

"*Now* it's started," he said. Then he and his gorilla goons headed off toward the field.

To be honest, I've never understood why Miller hates me so much. The only reason I hate him is because…well, because he hates me. I know I should have kept my mouth shut at that point. Obviously. But I'm not always so good at *should*.

"Hey, Miller!" I said. "What's your problem, anyway? What have you got against me?"

Miller just looked back at me once, shrugged, and kept on walking.

"Soon as I remember, you'll be the first to know," he said. "See you in school, buttwipe."

Yeah. That's exactly what I was afraid of.

NO COMMENT

When we got home, Grandma Dotty was making a big batch of Dotty's Meatballs for dinner. My grandmother and my mom can both cook like crazy, which is great because I can usually eat like crazy.

But not today. For once in my life, I wasn't hungry, even if the whole house did smell like one giant, delicious meatball.

"How did it go, kiddo?" Dotty asked.

"I don't want to talk about it," I said.

"Why?" my sister, Georgia, asked. "What happened?"

Anytime Georgia gets a whiff of bad news that has anything to do with me, it's like she turns into a bloodhound. She won't stop until she's hunted it down.

"I said I don't want to talk about it!" I told her. "Especially not to you."

"Me? What did I do?" she said, but I was already heading for my room.

Still, Georgia wouldn't quit.

"What happened?" I heard her asking Mom. "Is Rafe in trouble? Why is he so mad? What did Mrs. Stricker say?"

And that's when I exploded.

"SHUT UP!" I yelled all the way down the hall. "FOR ONCE IN YOUR LIFE, JUST SHUT YOUR STUPID NOSY MOUTH!"

Mom didn't even make me come back and apologize. The last thing I heard before I slammed my door was Georgia saying, "*Nosy mouth?* That doesn't even make sense."

Mom just said, "Let him cool off for a while. It looks like Rafe's had a hard day."

The truth is, my little sister was the *last* person I wanted to talk to about this. Georgia isn't that far behind me in middle school, and she's a total brain. So what would happen if she skipped a grade? Or if I kept blowing it the way I'd been blowing it?

It was actually possible that Georgia could wind up in the same grade as me! Or worse... MUCH WORSE...what if my little sister got out of middle school before *I* did???

So no, I did *not* feel like explaining to Georgia what had happened at HVMS.

And I didn't feel like eating.

And I *definitely* didn't feel like starting school that Monday.

Not only was I "special" now, but I was right back where I started with Miller too. It wouldn't be long before he found out about me being in the Learning Skills class. And I couldn't even think about what might happen then.

Mom's always telling me "Normal is boring," and that I'm an artist, and that I have all my own special talents, and blah-blah-blah. But none of that had gotten me anywhere except the reject pile with a bunch of other *kids like me*.

Whatever that meant.

The more I thought about it, the madder I got. I wanted to hit something. I wanted to *break* something. I wanted to go all rock star on my room and trash the whole place.

But I didn't. I just stayed put and did the one thing that makes me feel better when I'm stressed out. The one thing I'm halfway decent at.

I picked up my sketchbook and started to draw.

AND NOW FOR
MY NEXT BAD MOVE

That night was the first time I put any of my Loozer comics up online. Usually, I kept them to myself. But I guess I just felt like my art was the one thing I could do pretty well. The one thing that didn't make me feel so *special*, if you know what I mean.

I posted them on Art-Gunk.com, which is this random comics site I learned about when I went to art school in the big city. People could check out my stuff and make comments—good or bad. I didn't even use my real name. I said they were by some guy named R. K. Whatchamacallit, so no one would know who I was. I didn't think anyone at HVMS had even *heard* of Art-Gunk.com, much less cared about stuff like that.

But yeah, I know what you're thinking. Leo might not be real (more on him later), but how could I post a bunch of comics with a character called Loozer who looks like me and NOT think something bad was going to happen?

Well, I'll tell you the answer to that question right now.

And the answer is, I HAVE NO IDEA. I'm not exactly a world champion when it comes to looking before I leap.

So basically, without even knowing it, I'd started the clock on a brand-new time bomb, just waiting to go off. The only question was— when?

CHAPTER 7

MAYA, Dee-Dee, JONNY, AND Me

Okay, FLASH FORWARD! (You keeping up with me here?)

The first day of school was exactly what I expected—terrible.

Mrs. Stricker was standing by the front doors when I got there, yelling at everyone to go straight to homeroom. I think she threw up in her mouth a little when she saw me.

Of course, Mrs. Stonecase was standing right next to her. They're like the Twins of Terror, except they're not twins. Sisters of Suffering? Siblings of Sorrow? Family of Fe—

"MOVE ALONG, MR. KHATCHADORIAN!"

"Okay, okay," I muttered as I went in.

I also saw the super-crush of my life, Jeanne

Galletta, in the hall. When she asked me how it was going, I said, "Fine." She said, "Good." Then she left to talk to her stupid boyfriend, Jared "Perfect" McCall. For all the stuff he's so good at, I sure wish he was better at going to someone else's school.

I saw Miller the Killer too, but I don't think he saw me. It probably helped that I held my backpack up in front of my head when I walked by his usual hangout spot.

And all that was before I even got to first period!

My first three classes were English, math, and science. They piled on the homework too. Mr. Fanucci said I was supposed to bring all my assignments to Learning Skills, which was fourth period.

So while everyone else was taking World Languages or Computer Technology, I was heading down to the resource room in the library to find out who else was "special" like me.

I guess Mr. Fanucci works with different kids every period. There were only five of us in my group, which meant I couldn't exactly hide in the back. But it also means it won't take you very long to meet them.

This is Maya Lee. She has something nice to say about everything and everyone, all the time. Seriously. I'm not complaining, exactly, but after a while it's like, "Yeah, okay, I get it, Maya. You really like my pen. And my chair. And the way my shoelaces look." But at least she's nice.

Plus, she always brings homemade cookies for our group on Fridays. So I'm not complaining.

Hi, I'm Dee-Dee.
Nice to meet you.

This is Dee-Dee Molia. And to be honest, I kind of thought there would be more kids like her in our group. I think her brain works fine on the inside, but she needs a lot of help. She even uses an iPad to talk with, which is actually pretty cool. They let her sit in the front of every class so she can read the board. And when we have reading assignments, Mr. Fanucci makes sure they're all books she can listen to on her headphones. Sometimes I wonder if she's just listening to Taylor Swift or something. Hey, I couldn't blame her.

Jonny Hermenez knows a lot. And I mean a *lot*. As far as I can tell, the only thing he *doesn't* know about is how to get his homework done. But when it comes to stuff like why octopuses have three hearts, or how there are more than fourteen billion lightbulbs in the world, Jonny's got all that stuff down cold. If I'm ever on some game show and the million-dollar category is "Weird Little Facts," I'm calling Jonny for help, no question.

And this is me. You already know what I look like, but I figured I'd throw myself in here anyway. Maybe I'll never be best buds with Maya, Dee-Dee, or Jonny, but I don't think I'm any better than them either. I just wished I didn't have to take Learning Skills in the first place.

Meanwhile, if you're keeping track, you know there's one more kid in our group. Let's just say I saved the best for last.

FLiP OUT

About ten minutes after I met Philip "Flip" Savage, all I could think was, "What is *he* doing in this class?" He seemed totally normal and even pretty cool. But after another ten minutes, when Mr. Fanucci had to separate him for some "quiet time," I started to figure it out.

Flip is like a spinning top that never loses its spin. Like one of those gyroscopes that just goes, and goes, and goes, and goes...

...and goes, and goes...

...and goes.

He's also possibly the funniest person I've ever met. He's even funnier than that sit-down/stand-up comedian kid I heard about, Jamie Grimm.

For instance, I already told you Mr. Fanucci's first name is Edward, right? On the first day, Flip said, "Hey, Mr. Fanucci, can we call you 'Special Ed'?" That got a big laugh, so even when Mr. Fanucci said no, Flip kept going.

"Okay, we'll just call you 'Mr. Fun' for short," he said.

"I can live with that," Mr. Fun said. (And for the record, Flip calls him "Special Ed" when he's not around.)

Flip loves coming up with different names for everyone. He calls me "Short Stack" sometimes, because I'm half an inch shorter than him, plus I love pancakes. He calls Maya "Good News." Dee-Dee is "Gadget." And Jonny is "Factoid."

The other thing about Flip is that he's a total jock. Whatever nuclear power plant he's got running his engine on the inside, it makes him perfect for football, baseball, soccer, and lacrosse on the outside. (He's part of the reason I joined the football team, but more about that later.)

He even calls himself "Dumb Jock" all the time, which I think is hilarious.

He says that anything you can call yourself, it doesn't matter if other people call you that too, because you said it first. Which makes a lot of sense to me.

I'll tell you what else. This kid may not be very good at sitting still. And he's definitely not the world's best at math or English.

But I've never met anyone else besides Flip Savage that I just *knew* right away I'd be good friends with.

HOMe RUN
(BUT NOT THAT KiND)

As long as we're on the good stuff, I'll keep going.

Actually, it was more like a good news/bad news/good news kind of situation. First of all, I bumped into Jeanne Galletta right after school that Friday.

Like, actually *bumped* into her.

I had my head way down because the football team was just piling outside for practice again, and I wanted to look as un-Rafe-like as possible. Flip kept telling me not to worry so much about Miller, but Flip was Flip, and I was me. And Miller definitely had it in for ME.

Anyway, I was walking toward the bus, looking

at my feet, when—*BLAM!* All of a sudden, I was bouncing off someone, stumbling back, and hitting the dirt.

Jeanne hit the dirt too. The way she looked, it was like she hadn't seen me coming any more than I'd seen her.

"Rafe, I'm really sorry!" she said. "I wasn't even paying attention."

"Neither was I," I said. "Are you okay?"

And then we both just laughed. Which was kind of awesome, for about 3.2 seconds. I was thinking it might be a perfect moment for Jeanne to realize that she was meant to be my girlfriend, and for the two of us to move away somewhere— far away, where nobody was "special," and nobody got thumped in the chest just for being in the wrong place at the wrong time.

Or even better…maybe we could go somewhere far, *far* away, where there *were* no middle schools. Then I wouldn't have to worry about all those other problems either.

Yeah, that sounded pretty good. And maybe there could be a really cool beach too, where Jeanne and I could learn to surf together—

"Rafe?"

Jeanne waved her hand in front of my eyeballs, and I practically jumped.

"Huh?" I said. "I mean—sorry. What were you saying?"

"I just asked how your classes were going," Jeanne said.

Oh, man! The one thing I didn't want to talk to Jeanne about was how my classes were going. But before I could even change the subject, it got changed *for* me. That's when I heard that familiar voice, calling out behind me.

"Yo—KhatchaDORKian!"

Miller the Killer was closing in fast. I don't know what he had in mind, but I didn't want to find out either. So between that, and Jeanne asking all the wrong questions, I knew it was time to go.

"SeeyaJeannegottago," I said.

And then I ran. Like, *really* ran. Right past the buses, out onto Sylmar Avenue, and up the street headed for home.

Because you know how it is, right? Sometimes you have to hold your ground. Sometimes you have to face your fears.

And other times? You just feel like running.
So that's exactly what I did.

NeW ADDiTiON

When I came home that day, it seemed like nobody was there.

Except then I heard voices outside. Mom, Grandma, and Georgia were all in the backyard. When I got a little closer, I could hear Georgia complaining about something (of course).

"This is unfair! Not to mention irresponsible!" she said. "How could you do this to him? He doesn't deserve it!"

I stopped in the kitchen and listened through the door. I was the only *him* in our family. Which meant Georgia was talking about *me*. In fact, it sounded like she was sticking up for me about something. Which was weird.

Like, *really* weird.

"He's going to be fine," Mom said. "He just needs some love and care, like anything else."

I thought that was nice of Mom to say. But then it went back to weird again.

"I love his big ears," Dotty said.

My ears?

"Yeah, well, if he poops in my room, I'm calling the police!" Georgia said.

"Don't be so dramatic," Mom said. "If you don't want him in there, just keep your door closed."

"HEY!" I yelled. I was getting mad now. I mean, I know I'm kind of messy sometimes, but did they really think I was going to do *that* in Georgia's room?

"Rafe, is that you?" Mom said. "Come out here!"

"Everyone stop talking about me!" I was shouting...right up until I came outside. And that's when I got one of the biggest shocks of my life.

"Surprise!" Mom said.

I was kind of speechless. "Is that...?"

"It's a dog!" Grandma said.

"Well, yeah," I said, "but does he...?"

"I give it a week," Georgia said.

"I mean, is he...mine?"

"Yes, he's yours, Rafe," Mom said.

"This poor dog," Georgia said. "It's like giving a pet to a sloth. Or a mole. Or a—"

I didn't even hear the rest. I was already down on the ground saying hi to my new dog (!!!!) and getting licked all over my crazy grinning face with a thousand sloppy kisses all at once.

(And NO, that's not the "first kiss" I told you about in chapter 1. Give me a break!)

"We got him at the shelter," Mom told me. "His last family couldn't keep him, but he's already house-trained, and they said he knows a few commands too. Why don't you try some out?"

"Sit, boy!" I said, but the dog just looked at me.

"Lie down!" I tried, and he licked my shoe instead.

"Shake?" I asked doubtfully.

That's when he sat down.

"I guess we're not going to call him Einstein," Georgia said.

But I didn't care. So what if he wasn't the world's smartest dog? I'm not exactly the world's smartest kid.

Still, I did have one huge decision to make. What the heck was I going to name this little guy?

NAME THAT DOG!

I thought about calling him Zoom, after my favorite drink.

Then I thought about naming him Chunks, since he looked kind of like a meatloaf with legs.

Or maybe Mutt, I thought. Because he was definitely one of those.

Or Steve, because how many people have a dog named Steve?

But I just couldn't decide.

"Maybe you have to get to know him a little bit first," Mom said. "How about we all go for a nice walk?"

She even had the leash and a plastic bag all ready to go. A few seconds later, we were out the door and headed for the park.

This was going to be AWESOME! Maybe I didn't have a name for him yet, but I could tell he was going to be a great dog. And I was going to be a great dog-dad, or whatever you call it. I'd take him to the park every day. I'd take him to the woods. I'd take him *everywhere*. Someday, I'd have my driver's license and we'd *really* get to travel. Maybe start with the Grand Canyon, then a quick stop in Las Vegas on our way to Hollywood, Calif—

"RAFE!" Georgia yelled somewhere behind me.

When I turned around, Mom, Grandma Dotty, and Georgia were all standing there, looking at something on the ground.

"Use the plastic bag!" Georgia said. "That's what it's for."

And I thought, *Oh, right*. That too.

But even that wasn't so bad. You just have to breathe through your mouth when you pick it up. Then it's hardly gross at all. Warm? Yeah. Soft? Only if you grab it too hard.

I'm just saying—if you have a dog that you love, it's totally worth it.

Once we got to the park, there was a big open place where I could let him off the leash to run.

And you know what? That little meatloaf was
fast. Those four dog-sized legs of his were just as
good as my two human-sized ones, plus a little
bit more. I could barely keep up. By the time we
got back to Mom, Georgia, and Grandma, I was
about ready to throw up a lung.

"That was quick," Georgia said. "I guess what he doesn't have in brains he makes up for in speed."

Just like me, I thought. In fact, it kind of seemed like that dog and I were made for each other. Like he was just a small, four-legged version of me.

And *that's* when I finally figured out what his name should be.

Everyone, say hello to Junior, the best, not-quite-smartest, almost-fastest dog a kid could ever hope for.

LeARNiNG KiLLS

That first weekend with Junior went by faster than Christmas. We must have covered twenty miles, running all over Hills Village. It was the best weekend I've ever had.

And then, just like that—*poof!*—it was time to get back to school. (Don't you hate how that happens?) Back to math, science, social studies, killer bullies, killer food (not in the good way), and of course, Learning Skills with Mr. Fanucci.

"Good morning, everyone. I hope you had fantastic weekends," he said, just like last week.

"I'd give mine an eight," Flip said.

"Mine was super!" Maya said. "In fact, it was super-duper!"

"Did you know that the term 'weekend' didn't exist until the sixteen thirties?" Jonny said.

"I went to the science museum with my mom,"
Dee-Dee said through her iPad.

I didn't say anything because I was sitting
there thinking about where I wanted to take
Junior after school.

Flip had a pretty good nickname for Learning
Skills too. He called it "Learning Kills," and
here's why. At the beginning of every period, we
had to show Mr. Fanucci these notebooks he gave
us on the first day. In the notebooks, we were
supposed to write down every single one of our
assignments for every class, so we could keep
track of them. Then we had to check off one box if
the assignment was done, another box if we had
questions about it, another if it was late—

Just...kill...me...now.

Basically, it was like getting all the usual homework *plus* three extra periods a week for *thinking*
about homework, *talking* about homework, and
writing about homework. Which, by the way, is
exactly as boring as *doing* homework.

I mean, don't get me wrong. I'm not against
doing better in school. I'm just against getting
truckloads of extra work. (Mr. "Fun" says it's not

extra work, it's extra help, but he has to say that. He's the teacher.)

And none of that was even the worst thing about Learning Skills.

The worst thing was, we met in the resource room. It's a room off the library, and there's this big window in the wall in between. So anyone who was in the library during fourth period could see us sitting in there, being "special" with Mr. Fanucci. It was like spending fourth period in the zoo, if you ask me.

Not *at* the zoo. *In* the zoo.

Mr. Fanucci told us we shouldn't worry about those other kids. He said nobody was looking at us nearly as much as we thought. He also said that 99 percent of what we *imagined* people were thinking about us, they weren't thinking.

But I'm pretty sure they were.

And right after class that day, I got some proof.

PROOF

When I came out of Learning Skills, guess who was sitting right there in the library? Miller the Killer. Of course. He was at one of the computers, looking at meathead.com, or whatever it is he does with a computer. I didn't worry about it too much. Mrs. Seagrave was at the desk, and let's just say they don't call her the Bulldog of the Library for nothing. She'll bite your head off if that's what it takes to keep you quiet.

But just when I was ready for a clean getaway, Miller pushed back his chair. Then he planted himself between me and the door like a big, steaming pile of NOPE.

"What's up, Khatchadorian?" he said.

I noticed he didn't say Khatcha*dork*ian. But

even that seemed like a bad sign, somehow.

"Watch out, Miller, I've got to go," I said, like that was going to do me any good.

"What class is that?" Miller said, pointing at the resource room. He said it just loud enough so the kids at the other computers could hear too. But not Mrs. Seagrave.

"It's Learning Skills," I said, and tried to get past him again. "Watch out."

"Learning Skills? What's that?" he said, a little louder. A couple of people looked over now.

"You know what it is," I said.

"Oh, *riiiiight!*" he said, like he'd just remembered. "So I guess that means—"

"MR. MILLER, THIS IS NOT A SOCIAL CLUB," Mrs. Seagrave barked. "AND MR. KHATCHADORIAN, DON'T YOU HAVE SOMEWHERE TO BE?" (I swear, she's the loudest librarian you've ever heard.)

So I guess bulldogs can be useful sometimes. It got me out of there, anyway.

But the damage was already done.

See, I always figured I had two things on Miller. I knew he was bigger and scarier, and he could

pound me like a railroad spike. But I was faster. I could always outrun him if I had to.

And up until that day, I also thought I was smarter. (Not *smart*. Just smarter than Miller, which wasn't that difficult.)

Except—not anymore. Now that I was in Mr. Fanucci's class, my brain was officially dumber than Miller's. I knew it. He knew it. And worst of all, he knew I knew it.

And that stunk like an eight-week-old pile of fish guts sitting on the hot blacktop in the middle of August.

Plus just a tiny bit more.

THERE'S ALWAYS ART

The best part of my week was art class. I only
had it on Tuesdays and Fridays, but it was
with Ms. Donatello, which was cool.

When I started middle school, Ms. D was my
English teacher. I used to think that she was
the Dragon Lady and that all she wanted was to
make my life miserable. (Kind of like you-know-
who…Rhymes with Filler, Diller, and Chocolate-
Vaniller.)

But it turned out that Ms. D was okay. She's
the first person besides Mom who ever told me I
was a good artist. (She actually said "talented,"
but that's just embarrassing.) And she's the closest
thing I've ever had to a teacher being a friend.

This year, besides teaching English to the sixth
graders, she got stuck teaching art class for my

grade. Which is awesome for me, since she's practically the only grown-up in this whole school who likes me. Budget cuts can come in pretty handy sometimes.

So far, she'd been showing us all these famous works of art that she said every kid should be aware of. We'd talked about King Tut's funerary mask, the *Mona Lisa*, a painting of a diner called *Nighthawks*, and Andy Warhol's picture of a can of tomato soup (which I'm not so sure about, but Ms. D said it was "important"). And that wasn't all.

She seemed like she knew what she was talking about, anyway. And I knew I could trust her with something private, which was more than I could say about my other teachers at HVMS.

So at the end of class, I stuck around, taking a crazy long time to put my pastels away. But really, I was just waiting for everyone to leave. I wanted to ask Ms. Donatello a question. A really basic one.

I walked up to her desk, where she was drawing with a charcoal pencil. "Ms. Donatello, can I talk to you?" I said.

"Of course," she said. "About the assignment?"

"No," I said. "Not really. It's just that, um…well,

you've known me since I started middle school, and you can be honest, okay?"

Ms. D put down her pencil. "Okay," she said.

"I just need to know something," I said. "Am I dumb?"

"Excuse me?" she said.

"I know how that sounds," I said. "But seriously, not everyone can be smart, right? That's how it works. Someone has to be dumb. And I was just wondering if you thought—"

"I'm going to stop you right there, Rafe. Because I don't believe in 'dumb,'" Ms. D said. She even seemed a little mad. "Take a look around this room. What do you see?"

That wasn't what I expected. In fact, I wasn't sure what she was asking, which just made me feel—hello?—kind of dumb.

"Um..." I said, "the lock on that window's broken?"

"Look at the art," she said. She had pictures on the wall, of all those masterpieces I was talking about a minute ago.

"The people who created these were some of the greatest artists to ever live," she said. "They saw the world differently. And that means some of them probably learned things differently too. Just like you. I don't know what 'dumb' has to do with any of that, but I'd suggest you stop worrying about it."

"It'd be easier to not worry about it if I wasn't in Mr. Fanucci's class," I said.

"Yes, well, you *are* in Mr. Fanucci's class," she said. "You're also in mine. And I expect big things from you."

"You do?" I said. Because most people don't.

"Of course," she said, like it was obvious. "You shine brightly, Rafe. Sometimes on the outside, and always on the inside. Let's see some of that with your work this year, okay?"

I'll admit one thing. I left that art room feeling a whole lot better than I did when I came in.

But I also noticed Ms. Donatello didn't exactly answer my question either.

So I kept asking around.

CHAPTER 15

A FLIPPIN' BiG IDEA

ater that week, Flip was hanging at my house, and I figured I might as well get an expert opinion besides Ms. Donatello's.

"Hey, Flip? Do you think we're dumb?" I said.

"Definitely," he said.

Or more like shouted. Our house can be kind of noisy sometimes. Georgia and her "band," We Stink, were practicing in the garage. Dotty was running the vacuum cleaner in the living room. And Flip and I were in my room, playing one of my favorite new games with Junior. The game is called Drive the Dog into a Psycho Frenzy with a Laser Pointer.

Flip had the laser pointer, and Junior was running around my room trying to bite that tiny red dot on my blankets…my rug…my walls…my desk…my pile of dirty clothes. It's an awesome game.

"Why are you asking me that, anyway?" Flip said. He had the laser pointed at my pillow now, and Junior was going at it like we were one bite away from a room full of feathers.

"It's Miller," I said.

"Don't worry about Big and Tall," he said (which was Flip's name for Miller).

"I have to," I told him. "Miller has hated me since dinosaurs were working the drive-thru at McDonald's. And now this whole Learning Skills thing is just one more reason why he—"

"You know what you should do?" Flip said all of a sudden. Flip does *everything* all of a sudden. "You should get on the football team!"

He said it like it was the best idea ever. When actually it was kind of the opposite. I couldn't even imagine myself on the football team.

Actually, I *could* imagine it, but not in any kind of good way.

"Yeah, I'll get right on it," I told Flip. "Right after my next mission to Mars."

"I'm as serious as a goldfish funeral," he said. "Miller would *have* to respect you then. You'd be on the same team."

"There's just one problem with that," I said. "WE'D BE ON THE SAME TEAM!"

"Exactly," Flip said.

See? He wasn't getting it.

"I'll tell Coach Shumsky everyone calls you the Cheetah 'cause you're so fast," Flip said.

"They do?" I asked, impressed.

"No," he said. "But we could use another good runner this season. Coach likes to mix things up, and you usually don't see a lot of rushing TDs in flag ball, except on reverses, jet sweeps, or QB scrambles—"

"I don't know what any of that is," I said. I knew some about football, but it sounded like Flip was speaking a different language.

"I'm just saying, if you can run, Coach will at least let you suit up. It'll be great!" he told me.

"Forget it," I said, but Flip wasn't even listening anymore. Or at least, he couldn't hear me. Junior was licking the inside of his ear like it was filled with gravy, and Flip was laughing his head off.

Not that it mattered, because there was NO WAY IN THE WORLD I was going to be trying out for that football team. Not in a million years. Not in a *billion* years.

At least, that's what I thought.

But I've never been wronger.

CHAPTER 16

Q.T. Pie

If that whole football thing made me think Flip was crazy, the thing that happened next clinched it for sure.

I guess Junior had really cleaned out his ears, because right after that, Flip sat up and looked around.

"What's that music?" he said.

"It's not music," I said. I don't usually call We Stink a "band," because that would be an insult to bands everywhere.

"Let's go see," he said.

"Let's not," I said, but Flip was already heading outside. "Okay, but don't blame me if your brain starts bleeding," I told him.

We Stink usually practices in our garage. Mom brings a pie to the landlord, Mr. Tinker, every week, and he lets Georgia use the garage for practice. So I know what Mr. Tinker gets out of it (delicious pie) and I know what Georgia gets out of it (somewhere to practice). But meanwhile, all the rest of us have to listen to a group that—let's face it—calls itself We Stink for a really good reason.

Georgia plays the electric guitar, but she's never taken a single lesson in her entire life. Trust me—that becomes pretty obvious as soon as she plays her first note (if you can call it that). The other members of We Stink aren't much better.

So far, they'd played one and a half shows. One was a birthday party for Mari, the bass player. And the other was a bar mitzvah where the mom paid them extra to stop early. I'm not even kidding. My sister's like some kind of genius in school, but she's never going to get rich playing that guitar of hers.

Right now, they were in the middle of playing one of their "greatest hits." That's what Georgia calls them, so I guess she does have a teensy-weensy sense of humor about it all.

This one was called "What's the Square Root of U?" (Which tells you everything you need to know about my sister.) And it goes something like this:

Me minus you, equals nothing that I wan to do If we're divided, my woe multiplies But when we're together, the time just flies Oh yeah, oh yeah Plus ooh-ooh-ooh...

"Who's that girl playing guitar?" Flip shouted in my ear. "She's cuuu-ute."

I took a step away from him then, just in case whatever brain fever he had was contagious.

"Dude, gross! That's my sister," I said.

"You have a sister?" he said.

"Are you joking?" I asked him. "You've probably seen her at school a hundred times by now."

"Why didn't you ever tell me she was your sister?" he said.

"I don't know. It's like owning the fart in the room," I said.

The other part of the answer was that I didn't like people knowing my *little* sister was ten times smarter than me. But I didn't tell that to Flip. He was just standing there smiling at Georgia while she turned the color of a stop sign.

"Yeah, well, you know what?" he said, bopping his head like he actually liked the music. "That's one cute fart."

Ugh.

A LiTTLe BiT FAMOUS

That night, after Flip went home, I picked up my pencil and tried to draw. Usually ideas come really easy to me, but this time was different. Every time I came up with a good story for a Loozer comic, my mind would wander and I'd end up forgetting what I was supposed to draw.

Junior wasn't much help. When I asked him for an idea, he just wagged his tail and drooled on my pillow.

I don't know if it was the whole Miller business, or what Ms. Donatello told me, or everything Flip said, or Mr. Fanucci's class, but SOMETHING was distracting me. Actually, it was probably all four, because they were all bumping around inside my head like a bunch of zombies in a dark room.

I gave up and went online instead. I logged into Art-Gunk to see if my Loozer comics were still there or if they'd been banned for being too lame and boring.

And then something totally unexpected happened.

I saw that people were actually reading my comics! While I'd been busy making it through school all week, a bunch of people I'd never heard of had been checking out Loozer and Leo.

And I mean real, actual people. It wasn't a ton, but I did have seven comments waiting for me. Four of them weren't even that bad!

TurkeySandwich045
| COOL

GlitterKitty
| 👏 👏 👏

Axelrod_Dorlexa
| What-evs... 😑 z^z

CalvinHobbesFan
| This kid is sick.

Comixx4817
| Pretty good i guess

MangaFreak
| DummmmmmmmmMMmbbb

BugsFunny
| This is good, do more! ☺

The crazy wasn't over yet either. Not by a long shot. You'll see what I mean in a few more chapters, but meanwhile, four things happened just then.

One: I got nervous. It felt weird, knowing that my Loozer comics were out there in the world now and people were looking at them.

Two: I got excited. Because, well, my comics were out there in the world and people were looking at them.

Three: I couldn't stop reading those comments over and over. I must have read most of them fifty times each, plus another fifty times for the one that said, "This is good, do more!"

Four: I wanted to do more! Lots more! I spent the rest of that night drawing comics, and scanning them, and putting them up online.

Hey, I figured it was the least I could do for Loozer's die-hard fans.

All four of them.

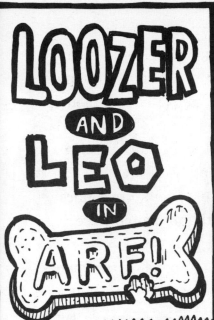

CHASE SCENE

If you know me, then you know a little about how my life usually goes. Just when I'm doing okay, something comes along and—*BLAM!*—blindsides me.

Or falls out of the sky.

Or walks up to me on the school steps and changes everything, just like that.

Which is what happened that Monday.

Right after the last bell, I was heading out for the day, and that's when I came face-to-face with Miller. Plus Tug Vincent. Plus Jeremy Savin. Also known as strike one, strike two, and strike three. I could tell something was up even before Miller called me Khatchadorkian.

"What's up, Khatchadorkian?" he said.

I tried to keep moving, but there were three of them and one of me.

"I've got to go, Miller," I said.

"Not if we get to you first," he said. And that's when they started closing in.

It was like it came out of nowhere. I didn't even know what I did this time—but it wasn't important. The important part was moving my feet, fast.

I was still standing in the door, and the only place to go was inside again. So I took off running up the hall and didn't look back. At least then if I got nabbed, Mrs. Stricker could give Miller a detention for staining the school floor with my blood and guts. Actually, she'd probably give him a trophy for that.

"You better ruuuuuuun!" Miller said behind me.

He didn't have to worry about that. I winged it past the music room, booked up the main hall, took a left just before the office, and kept right on going.

I hated running away, but it couldn't be any more embarrassing than whatever those three had waiting for me. Mega-wedgie? Target practice? Some new kind of cruel and unusual punishment?

Those were the things that kept me moving at absolute top speed.

When I got to the end of the hall, there was nowhere to go but outside. I tore open the door and cut around the back of the gym. I was thinking that the best way to confuse Miller was to keep turning corners. Back and forth, inside and outside, whatever it took.

I tried the first gym door—locked!

I tried the second gym door—locked!

Meanwhile, Mr. Big and Tall was closing in fast. So I gave up on the whole serpentine thing and went for a straight line out of there. But then—*SPLAT!* I plowed into Jeremy and Tug coming the other way.

I guess they'd split up, like those raptors in a *Jurassic Park* movie. Usually right before someone gets eaten.

"Don't let him go!" Miller said.

One of them grabbed me on the left. One of them grabbed me on the right. Then they picked me up off the ground and carried me over to where Miller was waiting.

At least he was huffing and puffing a little.

Maybe I'd worn him out enough so that the first punch would only be semi-fatal, instead of taking me all the way out.

But then again—I'm not usually that lucky.

HERE'S THE DEAL

I'm not going to lie. I was shaking in my boxers. I started wondering who was going to take Junior on his walks while I was in the hospital. And what color my casts should be. All four of them—one for each arm and leg.

"Hey, I'm talking to you!" Miller yelled.

"Huh?" I said. I guess maybe my eyes were just a tiny bit squeezed shut.

"I said, are you always that fast?" he asked me.

"Uh, yeah," I said, not sure if it was a trick question. "I'm always that fast."

"'Cause Flip said you're coming out for football."

And I thought—*Ohhhh*. That was what this was about. Miller wanted to make sure I didn't go anywhere near his precious team.

I had no problem with that.

"Flip's wrong," I said. "Don't worry. I'm not even thinking about going out for football. Seriously."

Miller took a step forward—then another. He put his face right up to mine. (My feet still weren't touching the ground, by the way. The goons still had me by the arms. I was 100 percent helpless, and about 80 percent going to wet my pants in a second.)

"Wrong answer," Miller said.

"We need some speed on the field," Tug told me. "And you just passed the first tryout."

I was like—*Huh???*

"So now you're going to convince Coach Shumsky to put you on the Falcons roster," Miller said. "Or else."

"Or else what?" I said.

Miller faked a punch then. And yes, I flinched like someone had just slammed on the brakes.

"Or else we go back to doing things the way we've been doing them," Miller said, grinning like an evil jack-o'-lantern. "Except maybe a little bit worse."

I think "worse" meant he was throwing Tug and

Jeremy into the deal, but it didn't matter. I got the drift either way.

"But if you're on the team, we've got no problem," Miller said.

In other words, I either played football or I took everything Miller (and Jeremy and Tug) could dish out, from now to the end of middle school—or until I was dead, whichever came first.

"So...you *want* me on the team?" I said.

"Wrong again," Miller said. "*You* want you on the team. From now to the end of the season, football is your life. Got it?"

Just then, the gym door opened and Coach Shumsky came outside, along with a bunch of other players. I saw Flip, and he looked at me like he was as confused as I was.

At the same time, Tug and Jeremy let me down, and I hit the dirt like a sack of Rafe-potatoes.

"What's going on out here?" Shumsky said. "Why aren't you fellas warming up like I told you?"

"Khatchadorian wants on the team, Coach!" Tug said.

"And he can run like his life depends on it," Miller said. Then he looked right at me. "Isn't that right?"

I spent about one and a half seconds thinking about all my possible answers. And then I realized there was only one.

"That's right, Coach," I said. "Please, please, please, can I play for the Falcons?"

CHAPTER 20

NOT EXACTLY A NEWS FLASH

So unless you just picked up this book and started reading here, you already know that I made the team.

Coach Shumsky said he wasn't offering any promises about putting me into the first game of the season, since I'd missed some practices. But I also saw the way he looked at Assistant Coach Flynn when I was running sprints during my tryout. I guess all those activities at Camp Wannamorra, killing myself in the Rockies, and running around town with Junior had paid off just a tiny bit.

The question is—did I *want* to play for the Falcons? And I guess that depends on what you mean by "want."

(That's half a pound of pure muscle!)

On the one hand, I've never been on a real sports team before. I didn't even know all the rules of the game yet. And I'm not exactly the most muscley, football-ready jock you've ever seen. More like the opposite. Don't get me wrong—I love playing sports, as long as it's with a controller in my hands and a couch under my butt.

But on the other hand, I figured this was still less risky than ticking off Miller. And Jeremy. And Tug.

Put it this way: If flag football was a five on a danger scale of one to ten, then those guys were somewhere around...oh, I don't know. Like a seventeen.

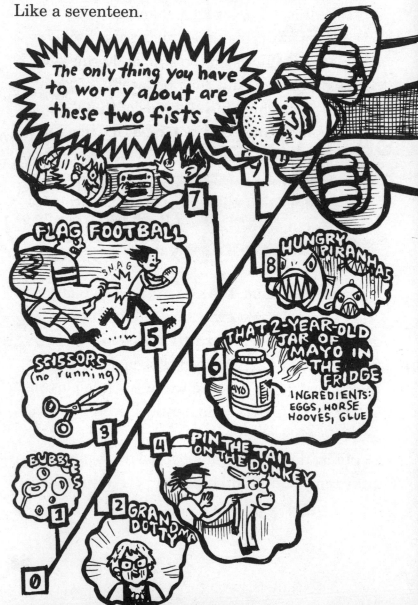

And when I thought about it like that, then I guess the answer was *yes*. I "wanted" to play football (aka stay alive) very, very much.

"Take this," Coach told me, and gave me a permission slip, plus some other papers to look at. "Have an adult sign the slip, and bring it to the next practice. And don't be late!"

Flip was flashing me all kinds of thumbs-ups by then, and Miller was looking at me like I'd just figured out a way to cheat death, which I guess I had.

But there were still a few more technicalities to go. Starting with one very big one.

I still had to get through Mom.

CHAPTER 21

GiVING MOM THe SLiP

That night at dinner with Mom, I felt like a real two-face. Or at least a one-and-a-half-face.

I didn't want to lie, exactly, but if I told Mom the whole truth about why I needed to join the football team, she probably wasn't going to sign that permission slip. She'd give me a big lecture about my "choices." And then she'd go talk to Coach Shumsky or Mrs. Stricker—or even *worse*, Miller's parents. All of that was just a one-way ticket back onto Miller's hit list.

So I had to think creatively.

"This is so sudden," Mom said. "You've never expressed an interest in football before."

"I've never had a best friend on the team before," I said. Which was true.

"What about school, sweetie? You've got all your classes, plus Learning Skills—"

"Flip is in Learning Skills. And he plays football," I said. Also true.

Mom was looking at me the way a detective stares down a shady suspect. "I don't know, Rafe. Why do I get the impression there's something you're not telling me?" she asked.

I wanted to say—*BECAUSE THERE'S TWO MORE TONS OF STUFF YOU DON'T KNOW ABOUT!* I wasn't telling her about my stupid deal with Miller, but I also wasn't telling her how dumb I felt in Learning Skills. Or how invisible I was to girls. Or how most of the kids at HVMS still thought I was just as big a loser as Loozer.

I don't know how long I could have lasted with Mom staring at me like that, but luckily, I didn't have to find out. That's when the doorbell rang. Talk about saved by the bell!

"I'LL GET IT!" Georgia yelled, and practically threw her chair across the room trying to get to the door first. My sister just *loooves* to answer things. Doorbells. Telephones. Math questions. It doesn't matter—she's an all-purpose answering machine.

A second later, she was back. "Rafe, your teacher is at the door."

"Huh?" I said, and I got this lumpy feeling in my stomach. A teacher coming all the way to your house is never a good sign. All I could think was, *What did I do now?*

I wondered if it was Ms. Donatello, but when Mom and I went to see, Mr. Fanucci was standing on the other side of the screen door.

"Hey, Rafe," he said, and held up my Learning Skills notebook. "You left this in my room today."

I don't know if he saw I'd crossed out the first S in *Skills*, but he didn't seem mad, anyway.

"Well, that was awfully nice of you," Mom said. "You shouldn't have gone to the trouble."

"It's better if Rafe keeps up with the notebook every night," Mr. Fanucci said.

Then Mom gave me one of her looks. The *told you so* kind.

"We were just talking about keeping up in school, weren't we, Rafe?" she said.

"Okay, well, thanks a lot, Mr. Fanucci," I said. I was trying to move this along, but Mom kept talking.

"In fact, I'm glad you're here, Ed. Rafe was asking about playing football, and I was saying I didn't think it was such a good idea."

I knew what Mom was doing. She was looking for some backup—but then Mr. Fanucci really surprised me.

"I think most of my students can benefit from extracurricular activities," he said. "And football could be a great outlet for you, Rafe. But not if your mom thinks it's a bad idea right now."

"It's not that," Mom said. "I just don't want him falling behind at school."

Mr. Fanucci gave this big smile. "That's what I'm there for," he said.

Mom smiled too. I just kind of stood there.

"How about if we make it provisional?" Mr. Fanucci said.

"What's that mean?" I asked him. It felt like we were moving in the right direction, but you know what they say about chickens and counting and hatching, right?

"It means you play only as long as your grades keep up. If they slip—no more football. And I'll work with you to make sure that doesn't happen," Mr. Fanucci said.

"I can live with that," Mom said. "How about you, Rafe?"

"Sounds like a deal," I said, because what else was I going to say?

I'd already dug my way into a hole with Miller the Killer. The only thing to do now was keep digging, not look back, and hope for the best.

'Cause, you know...what could *possibly* go wrong?

ALL THE HAIRY DETAILS

Okay, so this next part is awkward, even to write about. There were a few more things that needed to happen before I could play football. Stuff that has to do with science.

Well, okay, biology.

Well, okay, *puberty*. (There, I said it. Now you can just skip to the next chapter.)

See, I don't know about your school, but at HVMS they have these Tanner Scale tests. They tell whether you're ready to do stuff like play football against kids who are bigger than you. And by bigger, I mean more mature. And by more mature, I mean the guys whose voices have already started changing. Or who have hair under their arms. Stuff like that.

So if I wanted to play football, I had to take the tests. Whatever that meant, exactly.

I'm not going to go into details about what happened in there, but the nurse told Mom I was okay for playing football, anyway. At least that part was taken care of. Check!

But I wasn't done yet. There was still one more totally embarrassing thing to go.

After that, Mom took me over to What's Up, Sport? That's the big sporting goods store at the mall where we could buy a mouth guard and... some other things. Trust me on this one. If you can

HELLO, WHERE ARE THE ATHLETIC SUPPORTERS AND PROTECTIVE CUPS?

ever possibly help it, you DO NOT want to shop for this stuff with your mom.

When we got home from the mall, Mom asked if I had any questions about how to put those things on, but I told her I was all set. I just took that bag and headed for my room so fast, you would have thought I was trying out for the track team too.

The truth? I wasn't 100 percent sure about how that cup thing worked, but if I couldn't figure it out myself, I'd ask Flip later. Like when no one else was around.

And even then—maybe not.

CHAPTER 23

MILLER-FREE ZONE

It wasn't *all* bad.

The next morning when I was at my locker, Miller walked right by me. He didn't knock my books out of my hand, or shove my face into the locker, or *anything*. He just kept right on walking.

And in case you don't know how amazing that is, just imagine a lion in Africa somewhere. He's moving along the plain, looking for something to eat, and there's a gazelle hanging out by his locker—I mean, by the watering hole. That lion is hungry—you can see it in his eyes—and usually there's nothing he likes better than starting his day off with a couple of gazelle kebabs cooked extremely rare.

But not today. Today, that lion just keeps right on going, like maybe he's more in the mood for zebra. Or springbok. Or whatever else. And the gazelle just about passes out, he's so surprised.

That's how weird and unnatural it felt.

Still, I wondered if maybe it was just a fluke. Maybe Miller didn't notice me or something.

But after Learning Skills, it happened again. I was coming out through the library, and Miller was sitting at his usual computer. I was feeling a tiny bit lucky by now, so I tested it out.

"Hey, Miller," I said.

"Hey," he answered. He didn't even call me Khatchadorkian. He just kept on looking at the pictures on the screen in front of him. (Or maybe he was reading something, but I doubt it. This *is* Miller we're talking about.)

At lunch, I ate with Flip and got all the way through my fries without someone stealing them off my tray.

In the boys' bathroom, I was able to walk out with my underwear still where it was supposed to be.

In gym, Tug Vincent picked me second-to-last for another round of Mr. Lattimore's famous dodge ball. Second-to-last…*but not last!* I think even Mr. Lattimore was surprised.

It was like the best, easiest day of middle school I've ever had. And I thought—*I could get used to this.* Now I just needed to make sure things stayed that way. Whatever it took.

Miller's NEW To-Do List

1. Wake up
2. Punch pillow (just cuz)
3. Lift weights
4. Eat
5. Go to school
6. Make life miserable for ~~Khatchadorkian~~ someone
7. Eat some more
8. Beat on ~~Khatchadorkian~~ someone
9. Football practice
10. Before-dinner snack
11. Dinner
12. Don't do homework
13. Watch TV
14. 8,000 push-ups
15. Bedtime snack
16. ZZzzz... (dream about punching things)

ME REALLY, REALLY TIRED!
~~PRACTICE MAKES PERFECT~~

The day of reckoning came: my first real football practice. Flip told me some of what to expect, but I was still pretty nervous.

And it turned out I was right to be nervous. Those were two of the toughest, sweatiest hours I've ever had.

For the "warm-up," Coach had us do a bunch of jumping jacks. Then stretches. Then push-ups. And *then* we had to run four times around the track. That's one mile—which is a long way to go. I may be fast, but not for a whole mile. By the time I was *starting* my fourth lap, most of the team had already finished theirs.

And the problem with that is, when you bring up

the rear, everyone else is already waiting to move on to the next thing. So the guy who needs the biggest break is the one who doesn't get one at all.

After that, we did "starts and stances." I never knew there was so much to know about standing. I learned the two-point stance, the three-point stance, the four-point stance, and how to take off running from all of them. Flip said I'd get the hang of it, but mostly I was just getting tired and hungry.

We weren't done yet either. After that, Coach split us up into offensive and defensive squads. Since I was a runner, I got put on offense, and I spent the rest of practice trying to learn how to take my stance…start running…navigate around a whole bunch of moving bodies…watch for a ball that was coming from *behind* me…and more than anything, NOT let someone grab a flag out of my belt.

For any of you who don't already know, flag football is like regular football except for this belt you have to wear, with two flags on it. Getting one of those taken off of you is the same thing as getting tackled, but less painful. (Still, that didn't mean it was easy! Just the opposite.)

The first time I actually caught a pass, I was so excited, I forgot to run. Half a second later— *FWIP!*—someone grabbed one of my flags.

The next four times I tried, it didn't go so well. I dropped the ball. Then I took one in the face. Then I dropped it again. Then I missed it completely.

When I *finally* caught another pass, I was ready.

I turned around fast. I dodged once and got past Simon Bradtmiller. Then I got in two more strides downfield, right before—*FWIP!*

Coach blew his whistle. "All right, all right, let's go again," he said.

When I turned around, Miller was holding my flag in his hand. He was also giving me the Miller Glare. It's the thing that usually comes right before something even worse, like the Miller Fist.

"You're going to have to do better than that," he said. "A whole lot better, and right away. Else the deal's off." But he had his mouth guard in, so it sounded more like *"Yoth gon' haf doo be'ah'n'at....Who'lot be'er uh'rah'weh...elf fa dee's off."*

Still, I knew what he meant. This whole thing was going to get a whole lot harder before it ever got easier.

I mean—*if* it got easier.

And right now, that was looking like a mighty big IF.

CHAPTER 25

A LiTTLe HeLP?

"**W**haddja think?" Flip said. "Was that awe-some, or what?"

He smacked me on the back in the school parking lot, and it practically knocked me over. I was so wiped out. I already felt like one big rubber band from all that practice, but I didn't say so. I just tried to keep walking in a straight line.

"It was definitely...something," I said.

"So you're getting into it now, huh? I knew it," he said.

"Sure," I said. "Let's go with that."

I didn't tell him about the whole deal with Miller. It was too embarrassing. Plus, Flip still kind of thought *he* was the reason I joined the team.

"You want to stay over next Friday?" he said.

"Seriously?" I asked him. I'd never actually had a sleepover at anyone's house before. I'd barely had a best friend before, unless you count Leo, who's awesome but also, you know, imaginary.

"Sure," Flip said. "We can do extra training. You know—agility and catching and stuff."

That was his nice way of saying I was fast, but maybe not so good at everything else. Or anything else. Flip knew I needed extra practice. And now so did I.

"Sounds good to me," I said.

"Bring Junior too," he told me. "I've got an idea."

"What kind of idea?" I said.

"You'll see."

"All right," I said. "And, Flip? Thanks."

"No sweat," he said. But that was easy for him to say. Flip Savage was one part regular kid, one part machine.

As for me, I was pretty sure there *was* going to be sweat.

Lots and lots of sweat.

CHAPTER 26

BACK TO THE DRAWING BOARD

When I got home, even though I was worn out from practice, I still had to walk Junior. Then we had dinner. Then I had to do my homework and show Mom that I'd marked it off in my Learning Skills notebook. She wanted to see my art report for Ms. Donatello too.

Yeah, that's right. Ms. Donatello was making us do written reports—for art! That's kind of like making someone climb a rope for math class, if you ask me. But Ms. D didn't ask.

We were supposed to pick an artist, write a report, and then do an "art-class-worthy" cover for the whole thing. Ms. D was going to give one grade for the report and one for the cover.

I chose this guy named Jackson Pollock. He's one of Mom's favorite artists. I like how his stuff looks like a big mess, but everyone says he was a genius anyway. His most famous paintings are just drips and spatters of different colors, and they're also worth jillions of dollars.

For the report cover, I drew the guy's face with a soft pencil, just dark enough to see. Then I dripped different colors of paint for his eyes, his hair, and that kind of thing, to make a portrait.

Jackson Pollock
by
Rafe Khatchadorian

And even though I was so tired I wanted to fall asleep in my tray of carmine red, I really enjoyed making the cover. I guess if you love something, it never gets to be a chore. The best part was, when I showed it to Mom, she knew who it was right away. That made me feel good. Really good.

"I'm proud of you, Rafe," she said. "You're doing really well. And I'm glad Mr. Fanucci talked me into letting you play football. I can't wait to see a game."

"Uh-huh" was all I could say to that.

"You must be excited with the season getting ready to start," she said.

"Coach already told me he wasn't going to put me in the first game," I said. "Don't get your hopes up. I'm still kind of playing catch-up."

"Oh, you'll be in there before you know it," Mom said. "Don't you worry, sweetheart."

"Uh-huh," I said again, because I didn't know what else to say. I mean, I *was* worried, but not in the way she thought. The idea of actually playing in a real football game made me want to shake right out of my socks...and then throw up inside them.

Maybe I was wasting my time. Maybe it was crazy to think I could pull off this stupid "arrangement" with Miller. Maybe the only thing that was going to get rearranged in the end was my face, either by Miller when I failed or by the other teams that were going to clobber me on the field.

The problem was—as usual—I had no idea what

the right thing to do was. Even though I wasn't
really enjoying football, I couldn't just quit it. Not
when it was basically a Get Out of Punches Free
card from Miller. But I couldn't really imagine ever
liking it....It didn't make me feel happy the way
drawing did, just worried. I'd never be a jock like
Flip. Or even half
the jock he was.

Dude! Couldn't you at least have drawn my good throwing arm?

And since I'd already decided I couldn't talk
to anyone else about all this, I did something I
hadn't done in a while. I waited until I was alone
in my room, and then I had a long talk with my
original, number one best friend.

Good old Leo.

CHAPTER 27

GOOD ADVICE

I know Leo's not real and all that, but I'll tell you what else. Some of the best conversations I've had in my life have been with him.

The sad part of that story is that the real Leo is my brother who died a long time ago. But I always kept him around anyway, at least inside my head. Mom says Leo's my muse now, which means he's good for ideas. Mostly, I've been putting him into my Loozer comics, but it doesn't matter how long it's been since we talked. He's always right there when I need him.

"Okay, so am I totally messing up?" I asked Leo. "Or is this a good thing?"

It didn't even take a second for him to answer. He always just knows stuff.

"It's a good thing," Leo said. "Miller's going to leave you alone now. That's huge."

"What about the football?"

"What about it?"

"I'm not sure I want to keep doing it, but Miller would kill me if I quit. And what if I *can't* do it?" I said. "What's the plan then?"

"You want to know the plan?" Leo said.

"I just asked you for it."

"Okay, here it is. It's called 'don't do anything.'"

"What does that mean?"

"It means, in case you hadn't noticed, you're not getting into trouble. You're not breaking any rules—"

"For once," I said.

"—or even *trying* to break the rules. You're just playing football, drawing your comics, hanging out, and going to school. That's called normal, dude. Try to relax."

Usually, Leo's all about one kind of scheme or another. He always has an idea about how I can make things more *interesting*. Now he was telling me to do nothing? It was weirder than weird.

But that's not the same thing as bad. Sometimes weird is good. And sometimes it's *really* good.

This is why talking to Leo is better for me than just about anything. I know it's all inside my head, but somehow, when I think about it that way—like it's me and Leo together, not just me on my own—it helps.

And I mean *always*.

CHAPTER 28

WHAT'S THE BIG IDEA?

I couldn't sleep that night. I was tired, but I just kept lying there, staring at the ceiling.

What Leo told me made sense, but there was something off that I couldn't figure out. What was it? I hadn't gotten into trouble for a while, Mom was pretty happy, and Mrs. Stricker might even have forgotten she hated me by now.

You have amnesia. Do you remember your name?

No. The only thing I can remember is I **HATE** KHATCHADORIAN!

Okay, maybe not that last part.

Around midnight, Mom told me to turn off my light once and for all, so I did. But then I just kept right on *not* sleeping.

The next time I looked at my clock, it was ten after one. Then one thirty. Then one thirty-eight.

And then I was up again.

"Junior?" I whispered. He's always ready for anything, so I put on his leash and we went outside for a walk.

And by outside, I mean our backyard. Mom would cancel my subscription to life if I went walking around the neighborhood at one thirty-eight in the morning. So we just went around and around and around the yard instead—like for forty-eight laps. (It's not a very big yard.)

So there I was, going in circles with Junior in the middle of the night, trying to get sleepy…and that's when it hit me.

I wasn't happy.

I know that doesn't seem like a huge revelation. It probably seems like I wasn't grateful for the cool stuff I had, like a dog and a best friend. I was, but Mom says outside things don't really make you happy inside (she usually trots that line out whenever I ask her for expensive sneakers or video games).

So why wasn't I happy? Things were good, as Leo said, and I could even learn to live with football and Learning Skills. And since I'm not the sharpest knife in the drawer, it took a few more laps with Junior to figure out what was wrong: football. And Learning Skills.

Yeah.

I could learn to live with them, but I wouldn't be doing them if it were up to me. I didn't make the choice to *join* them and I didn't have the choice to *quit* them. And that was the real problem. Hardly anything about my life, except for my art, was *up to me*. And that's what made me not-happy...and a little bit mad.

I stomped around the yard a few more times, getting more angry the more I thought about it.

Then something strange started to happen. In a good way. Mom says she gets some of her best painting ideas when she's mad. Maybe that's what happened to me.

At first, it was just this teeny-tiny little baby idea in my head. Not even that. Mostly, I was thinking about all those genius works of art in Ms. Donatello's classroom, and how she was expecting "big things" from me, and how she was barking up the wrong kid on that one.

Also, if you know me, then you know I once had a really gigantic idea at Hills Village Middle School, and it was something I thought of all by myself. Okay, Leo had a big hand in it, but he's technically a part of me. It was even called Operation: R.A.F.E., which stood for "Rules Aren't For Everyone." And even though I got in a lot of trouble for it, it was *my* idea. My choice.

Now I was thinking maybe I could do something big like that again. How crazy would that be? And unlike football or Learning Kills, the idea would be 100 percent *mine*.

The more laps I did around that yard, the more excited I got. I was going to take a little bit of what Ms. Donatello said, a little bit of R. K. Whatchamacallit, and even a little bit of Operation: R.A.F.E. Then I was going to throw it all in the blender and turn it into a whole new thing, like a giant smoothie made out of ideas.

Kind of.

Best of all, I already had a really good name for it. This one was going to be called Operation: S.A.M. And in case you're wondering (I know you are!), S.A.M. stood for:

It was time to get started.

CHAPTER 29

STROKE OF GENIUS

My mind was flying by the time I took Junior back inside. I grabbed one of Mom's big art books off the shelf and took it straight to my room. I definitely didn't feel like sleeping now. Operation: S.A.M. was practically pouring out of my brain.

So you know what Loozer looks like, right? I decided that SAM was going to be the opposite of him—filthy rich, crazy good-looking, and very, very stealthy. He was also a secret agent, and his mission was about putting great works of art all over Hills Village Middle School.

Not *my* art, exactly. But also, kind of, yes. You'll see.

I decided to kick things off with one of Mom's favorite paintings: *The Starry Night*, by Vincent van Gogh. He's one of those geniuses Ms. Donatello was talking about earlier. So I opened up that giant art book to a picture of the painting, and put it on my desk. Then I tore four pages out of my sketchbook and taped them together into one big sheet.

I wasn't sure how long this was going to take, since I'd never done it before. I just knew that I wanted to finish in time to be at HVMS really, really early—like right after the first janitor and before anyone else. So even though it was about two thirty in the morning, I just kept on working.

I pulled out my best pen, took a good long look at that crazy, swirly, genius masterpiece, and started to draw—*The Starry Night*, by Vincent van Gogh.

By SAM.

CHAPTER 30

SAM

I am SAM, and this is my first mission. Wish me luck.

Actually, don't bother. I'm *that* good.

I need to move fast, but I have to be careful too. This high-tech fortress disguised as a middle school has security systems like Hershey, Pennsylvania, has chocolate.

My biggest concern (and archnemesis) is Jan I. Tor. He's the half-human, half-cyborg "cleaning service" they use for "light security" around here.

Yeah, right. Tor's definition of "light security" is that he only kills you once if he finds you.

So I wait in super-stealthy silence while Tor hovers past my hiding spot with his motion detectors running, laser cannons loaded, and a big dust mop attachment on his robotic arm. He's cleaning that floor to within an inch of its life, but it could be me next.

As soon as Tor's out of range, I slip off my tungsten gripper shoes. Believe me, once he's been through here, you do *not* want to leave footprints behind. That would be like leaving a business card in Sergeant Stricker's in-box. Stricker is the big cheese who runs this place, and she's all human, but just as scary as Tor. I don't want to rumble with either one of those two. So I program the shoes to self-destruct and drop them in the trash. *FWOOM!*

The coast is clear now, and I sneak back into action. I work my way up the corridor in my spy socks, quiet as a ghost walking on cotton balls. Very, very puffy cotton balls—I'm *that* quiet.

What I need is the perfect place to leave the package I came here to deliver. That's the mission, but I can't just do it anywhere. I have to choose wisely.

Bathroom? Nah. Too echoey.

Library? Nah. Only one exit, and I can't take that risk.

Main lobby? Hmm...maybe so. In fact, I wish I'd thought of that on my way in. I could have saved myself one very expensive pair of tungsten gripper shoes.

Once my radar-enabled Rolex watch tells me the main lobby is clear, I slide in there and get right to work. I enter the access code on my brief-case, confirm with my thumbprint, and then pop the case open. After that, it takes exactly seven seconds and one ordinary roll of masking tape to secure my package to the wall.

That's it. Package delivered. Mission accomplished.

Catch you next time—because there's no way *you'll* ever catch *me*.

SAM out!

CHAPTER 31

ART SHOW

Getting in and out of school after the janitor opened up was easier than I thought. Once I did my whole Secret Artist Man thing, I just snuck back outside, walked around the block a few times, and came back as soon as the buses and parent drop-offs start to show up.

My grandma likes to watch a lot of old crime show repeats, like *Mulgroove & Bates*, and *Order and Law: Boston*, and *Order and Law: Toledo*, and *Order and Law: Canine Unit*. And I swear, on every one of those shows, the bad guy either shows up at the scene of the crime to see how everyone reacts, or else the good guys talk about how they have to keep their eyes open because the bad guy might show up at the scene of the crime to see how everyone reacts.

Which is where I got my idea for how to pull off the next part of Operation: S.A.M.

First I came strolling into school like everyone else. Then I stopped near the main lobby doors and got a drink of water.

Then I stopped next to the drinking fountain to tie my shoe.

Then I untied my shoe, got another drink, and tied my shoe again. (There's more, but you get the idea.)

That whole time, everyone was walking through the lobby. They all headed off in a million different directions while I just stayed to the side and watched. And listened.

Okay, if you want to know the truth, about 99 percent of the other kids didn't say anything. But they *all* saw that drawing, for sure. And at least six or seven of them said something about SAM. Like "Who's SAM?" Or "SAM who?"

I'd call that mission accomplished. Plus, I really liked being the only one who was in on the secret. I liked it a lot.

And speaking of people noticing, it didn't take long for Mrs. Stricker to figure out something was

up. She can smell trouble from two hundred yards, blindfolded. And she definitely knows when there's something hanging on the wall of *her* school that wasn't there before.

As soon as she walked through the lobby, it was all over. *FOOSH!* She sucked that picture off the wall like it was a ball of dog hair and she was the Vacu-Stricker 2000.

I didn't care, though. It was already mission accomplished (for now). I just took my extra-well-tied shoes and beat it before Mrs. Stricker could figure out I was anywhere within a mile of that art. It's not like I had broken any official rules, but why take chances? I wanted to live another day.

And so did SAM.

CHAPTER 32

SLEEPOVER BOOT CAMP

That Friday night, I showed up at Flip's house with a sleeping bag, a pillow, a toothbrush, and Junior. Mom made me bring the toothbrush.

"My dad's making bacon burgers," Flip said. "You picked the right night to come over."

I didn't pick the night at all, but who cared? If dinner was going to taste as good as it smelled, I was already glad to be there.

But first, Flip was going to make me work for it.

We started off just playing catch in the backyard. Flip showed me how to use my fingertips and how to keep my eye on the ball. I've heard people say that a million times before: *Keep your eye on the ball*. But guess what? If you actually do it when you're trying to catch, it helps.

"Now let's make this a little more interesting," Flip said. He went into the kitchen, where his dad was cooking. A minute later, he came out with something in a paper towel. He was also carrying a big roll of silver duct tape.

"Something smells like bacon," I said.

"That's 'cause it *is* bacon," he said. Junior was jumping up and down trying to get at it, but Flip held it over his head.

"You've heard of flag football, right?"

"Yeah," I said.

"And then there's Drive the Dog into a Psycho Frenzy with the Laser Pointer, right?" he asked me. "Well, this is like both of those combined, but instead of flags, we're using bacon. And instead of a laser, we're using you."

"Huh?"

"Turn around and raise your arms."

A minute later I had four pieces of bacon duct-taped around my middle, hanging down like football flags. Junior was drooling all over the grass while Flip held him back.

"You need to run across the yard, touch that tree over there, then come around that pine, over that rock, and back here without letting Junior get a taste of that bacon," Flip said. "Got it?"

It was pure Flip. One part hilarious and one part totally smart. I mean, we could have done it without the bacon—or without Junior—but what fun was that?

Flip gave me a ready-set-go, and I took off across the yard with Junior behind me, jumping up and snapping at my "belt." By the time all that bacon was gone, I'd made five full laps around the yard. Not bad. I'm not sure if it made me any better at football, but it sure made me laugh a whole lot. Junior liked it too.

And the night was just getting started.

CHAPTER 33

FACE YOUR FEARS

After all those rounds of baconball, I was ready for some bacon of my own. Dinnertime! And let me tell you something—Flip's parents know how to eat. I had two burgers, extra bacon, and thirds on cole slaw, corn bread, and chocolate pudding after that. It was awesome.

That night, we slept downstairs in the basement and talked for a long time. Flip told me about how he had to take medication for his ADHD. I told him about how I got kicked out of HVMS the first time, and basically flunked out of art school after that.

I didn't mind telling him some of my secrets. Just not all of them. Not the most embarrassing ones—like how afraid I was of Miller, or how I still hung out with my imaginary friend. Maybe I'd tell him all that sometime, but not yet.

Then, after midnight, when his parents went to bed, Flip told me there was one more part of my training.

"Football is all about facing your fears," he said.

"What's that mean?" I asked him. He reached under a couch cushion and pulled out a box. When he held it up, I saw it was a movie.

"*Hideous 2*," he said. "If you've got the nerve."

"I never saw *Hideous 1*," I said. "My mom doesn't like me watching R-rated movies."

"Same here," Flip said. "So we'll keep the sound down low. I mean...unless you're afraid."

Yeah, right. Like I was afraid of a dumb movie about people being possessed and turning into sizzling piles of acid when they were exposed to sunlight. I wasn't afraid. No way.

I mean, not until the movie really got going. But I wasn't going to admit that to Flip either.

So trust me on this one. If you've never eaten cold leftover burgers in the middle of the night while watching the scariest movie you've ever seen with your new best friend and your dog, then you're missing out.

MORE, PLEASE!

As busy as I was with football practice and hanging out with Flip, I made sure to keep my secret project, Operation: S.A.M., going the whole next week.

I never put two pieces in the same place either. The trick was figuring out how to put stuff up when no one was looking. Once I started paying attention, it wasn't that hard.

That night, I did a picture of this cool painting called *St. George Killing the Dragon*. I hung that one on the pull-down map in Mr. Frommer's classroom. Then during social studies, all I had to do was wait for him to start talking about the Holy Roman Empire, and—*BAM!*

Or I guess I should say—*ART!*

This time, I heard someone say, "Again?" And someone else said, "Okay, now I'm interested." Plus, Mr. Frommer took my drawing down and left it on his desk, which was better than getting it sucked up by the Vacu-Stricker 2000.

The next day, I was really getting into it. I drew a painting called *The Last Supper* and put that one up in the cafeteria. *Way* up.

Last Supper…cafeteria…get it? Because with the food at HVMS, you never know which meal might be your last.

Mrs. Stricker got the janitor to take my drawing back down, but I actually heard some kids booing when he did. That was cool to hear.

Then I tried something different. I drew the little angel guys from *The Sistine Madonna*, by Rafael Sanzio (the artist Mom named me after, if you want to know). Then I made a bunch of photocopies and put them up in a bunch of different places. Most of those didn't survive through second period, but I did find one still up in the bathroom during lunch. And I knew *someone* had noticed it, because they added their own little touch. Which I didn't even mind.

For Friday, I drew a painting called *The Scream*, by Edvard Munch, who has a great name, if you ask me. I like the painting too—but not as much as I liked what I did with it.

By the end of the week, HVMS had a real live mystery on its hands. I'd hear people in the hall saying stuff like "Did you see what SAM did today?" and "Why is he doing this?" and "How can one person be so good-looking, rich, and smooth?" (Well, two out of three, anyway.)

I wasn't exactly sure what was supposed to happen next, but I definitely wasn't stopping. I was having too good a time for that. And nobody had a single clue about who was behind it either.

At least, that's what I thought.

BLENDING IN

That day in art, Ms. Donatello had a question for all of us.

"How many of you have seen these 'SAM' drawings around school this week?" she asked.

(Awesome alert. Stand by for awesome.)

Every single hand went up. (Awesome!) And of course, I raised my hand along with everyone else, because: (1) I *had* seen those drawings, and (2) *duh*. It's called blending in.

"Can anyone tell me the name of the painting that was depicted on the flagpole this morning?" Ms. Donatello asked next.

Nobody knew, and I sure wasn't going to tell them. I just shrugged my shoulders like I'd never thought about it.

For a while after that, Ms. D talked about *The Scream*, and Edvard Munch, and then I'm not sure what else because my head was too busy exploding from the inside. I was loving every single second of this. And my cheeks were getting the workout of a lifetime, just trying not to smile.

But then after class, Ms. Donatello threw me a little curveball.

"See you Monday, Rafe. Keep setting those sights high," she told me. "And try to stay out of trouble, okay?"

It was the kind of thing she said all the time. Except this time, there was something about the way she said it, like it was code for something else. It made me wonder if she'd been talking about SAM for a reason. Like maybe Ms. Donatello was even smarter than I thought.

Or maybe SAM wasn't as stealthy as I thought. Or both.

Either way, it was like I said before—why take chances? I was going to have to be more careful than ever from now on.

CHAPTER 36

GAME FACE

Before I knew it, we were at game day. First game of the season! The team was all suited up. Mom was there. Mr. Fanucci was there. Jeanne Galletta was there. *Everyone* was there.

Once we did our warm-ups, they introduced the team over the loudspeaker, and all the guys ran through this giant piece of paper that said GO, FALCONS! Or at least, the guys at the front did. I was at the back, so I just ran over some little scraps of paper by the time I got there.

After that, it was time for the game to start. And I'll admit it—I didn't mind taking a nice safe seat on the bench one little bit. I'd already told Mom she shouldn't bother coming, since Coach Shumsky wasn't putting me in. But she said she wanted to be there anyway. When I looked up in the stands, she was sitting with Georgia and Grandma, waving these Falcon banners like they were born football fans.

The game was against our archrivals—Southside Middle School. But nobody expected us to win. Hills Village never beats Southside at anything. And while I sat there on that bench and the game got going, I started thinking about what a weird concept that is. I mean, how can another school—basically buildings and lawns and a parking lot—be our archrival?

Then after a while, I started thinking about some other stuff, like what I wanted to draw next for Operation: S.A.M. It was going to be something different—a picture of *The Thinker*, which is this cool sculpture by a guy named Rodin. I kind of wished I had my sketch pad with me, since I was getting some good ideas and I had all this time on my hands—

"OOOOHHHHH!"

That was the sound the crowd made all of a sudden. And I realized I hadn't exactly been paying attention. When I looked up again, the scoreboard said VISITORS: 21 HOME: 0. Southside was kicking our butts, no surprise.

But that wasn't all. Something had happened on the field. Flip was limping, with his arm around Assistant Coach Flynn's shoulder for support. Tug Vincent was holding his own arm against his chest. And our quarterback, Michael Alvarez, had an ice pack on his head.

I guess flag football was rougher than I thought. I'd been too busy up inside my head to even realize what was going on. Now three of our best players were out, and the crushing by Southside was *really* going to start. I even felt sorry for the guys Coach was going to send in next, because from the way Flip, Tug, and Michael were looking, it didn't seem like—

"KHATCHADORIAN! ARE YOU PAYING ATTENTION?"

Ooops! (That's kind of a bad habit of mine.) This time when I looked up, Coach Shumsky was pointing right at me.

"What's up, Coach?" I said.

"I'm not going to tell you twice," he said. "Take that jacket off and *get in there!*"

My heart felt like it had just started playing a little tackle football of its own, right inside my chest.

"Me?" I said.

"You know any other Khatchadorians around here?" he said.

People were cheering for the guys who had just come off the field—and also for the ones who were about to go in. *Including me!*

And as I got up onto my feet, all I could think now was—*Welcome to the meat grinder.*

CHAPTER 37

HERE GOES NOTHING

People were cheering and yelling when I stepped out onto that field, but I couldn't hear it anymore. All I could hear was that siren inside my head—the one telling me to run, duck, take cover, and GET OUT OF THERE! My knees were shaking for real, and I wondered if I was going to throw up on the ground, on my shoes, on the other players, or all of the above.

Even if I didn't get hurt, I was definitely going to humiliate myself. In front of everyone. Including Jeanne.

"Coach, I...I don't think I can," I said.

"Kid, it's just football," Coach Shumsky said. "This is your chance to go have some fun."

"Um...okay—"

"I'm kidding," Coach said. "Get in there. Go get 'em. You know the drill. Sic 'em!"

Ha-ha. *What a funny guy*, I thought. Coach Shumsky was a real comedian. Because anyone who thought this was going to be fun was a COMPLETE JOKER!

But I still had to get in there. No turning back now.

I joined the huddle with a couple of other subs. Miller took over for Tug at quarterback, and he already had the play from Coach.

"Baines, Harrison, Abuja, start wide and go deep. They've got their biggest guys in the middle. Let's see if we can get around them."

"What about me?" I said.

"Block number eighteen," Miller said.

When I looked up, I could see a guy with a big 18 on his back, huddling with the Southside team. As far as I could tell, this kid was somewhere between the size of an eighth grader and a house.

"Can I trade for someone else?" I asked Miller, but it was too late.

"We'll go on two," he said. "Break!" And just like that, we went into our positions.

Now that I could see number eighteen up close, he looked like a cross between a jackal and a serial killer. And I was pretty sure he could wad me up and toss me like a paper towel if he wanted to.

I mean, you're not allowed to *actually* tackle anyone in flag ball, but let me put it this way: How would YOU feel if someone told you to block THIS?

I couldn't remember what kind of stance I was supposed to do, so I just bent my knees and waited for the play to start. Or more like, prayed for it to be over fast.

"Rover twenty-three!" Miller said. "Hike! Hike!" I was probably supposed to know what that Rover thing meant too, but there was no time to think about it. Jason Carmichael made the snap, and everything started moving at once.

I'll give myself credit for this much—I actually reached for the big guy. I tried to stay low like I was supposed to, but I think I closed my eyes for a millisecond. By the time I was done blinking, number eighteen had done some kind of spinning twisty thing, right past me. He was heading for Miller, who still had the ball, and I thought, *Well, I tried*. Sort of. Hopefully it would be over in about a second.

And *that*, my friends…THAT…is when the unthinkable happened.

Miller grinned—he actually smiled—right before he threw me the ball. It came like a spinning time bomb, right at my head, and right through some kind of hole that hadn't been there a second ago.

All I could think was…actually, I thought a whole lot of stuff, but it all happened at the same time.

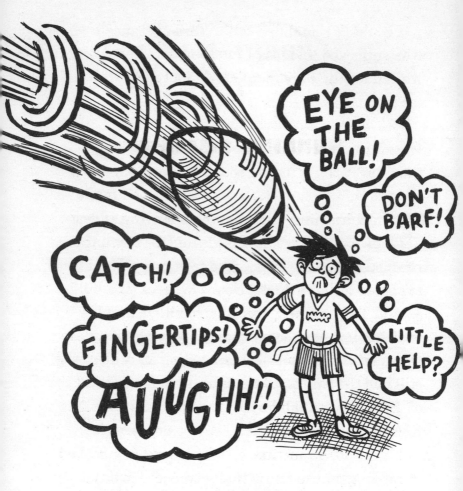

So, which one of all those things do *you* think won out?

(Hint: It might not be the one you expect. Keep reading and find out.)

RUNNING SCARED

The first thing I got moving was my hands, believe it or not. It wasn't pretty, and no, there were no fingertips involved—but just like that... I'D CAUGHT THE BALL!

And even crazier, I didn't drop it!

If I could have, I would have played hot potato with Miller and tossed it right back. But that wasn't going to happen.

"RUN!" I could hear Coach screaming. "RUN, KHATCHADO—"

I didn't hear any more, because my feet kicked in next. All those Southside guys were looking at me like I was dinner and they hadn't eaten in days. So yes, I took off running like I was supposed to.

It's just too bad I ran in the wrong direction.

"NOOOOOO!" pretty much everyone screamed at the same time, except for the other team. I kept expecting one of those flags on my belt to get whipped out, but so far, it hadn't happened. When I caught sight of Coach Shumsky on the sidelines, his face was somewhere between Smurf blue and plum purple. His scream was so high by now, I would have needed dogs' ears to hear it.

I heard Flip, though. He was on the bench and yelling one word over and over, plenty loud enough.

"BACON!" he screamed. "BACON! BACON! BACON!"

So I just kept on moving.

I'm not sure what made me run backward next, but I don't think anyone was expecting that. It got me headed toward the right end of the field, anyway.

Then I ran sideways. I zipped. I zagged. I turned and zagged again, like Junior was about to bite my heels off.

And that's when I saw a little slice of daylight, right between two of those giants from Southside. It was just enough for skinny little me to squeeze through.

After that, all I could see was the end zone at the far end of the field, about a mile away. (Okay, maybe more like forty yards.)

And I just kept on running.

All I could feel now was my legs pumping. All I could taste was the blood in my mouth (I bit my tongue when I caught the ball—oops). All I could hear was the crowd in the stands—and they were cheering for ME!

If I hadn't been there myself, I wouldn't have believed it. In fact, I still don't believe it.

But it was true.

CHAPTER 39

TOUCHDOWN!

Ten yards to go…
nine…
eight…
seven…
six…
five…
four…
three…
two…
one, and—
TOUCHDOWN!
KHATCHADORIAN SCORES!
RIGHT BEFORE HE DIES OF SHOCK!
I couldn't believe it. Like, actually couldn't
believe it. I kept wondering when Georgia was

going to start shaking me and yelling at me to wake up, because this had to be a dream, right?

Rafe Khatchadorian. Had just scored. A TOUCHDOWN.

Don't worry, I'm not going to keep saying it over and over again. It just took me a second to figure out that it was really happening. That was right about when Flip jumped on my back and started screaming, "Hills Village SCOOOOOOORES!!!" and "KhatchaDOOOORian!" and "YEEEEAH, BABY! TOUCHDOWN!"

The whole team piled on after Flip. I didn't just get congratulated. I got *mugged*. Seriously. It hurt. I guess there's no rule in flag football about tackling your *own* players.

But I didn't mind. It was still one of the best things that had ever happened to me, just in a slap-on-the-back, punch-in-the-arm, break-a-few-ribs kind of way.

I know, it's not like we won the Super Bowl or anything. But the thing is, Hills Village hadn't scored against Southside since…ever. So it was kind of a big deal. Which made *me* kind of a big deal for a minute there.

Were we still going to lose the game? Well, put it this way: Does a bear poop in the woods? Yes and yes.

But no matter what happened after that, nobody could ever take those six points away from me. Not even Mrs. Stricker and Mrs. Stonecase. And for the first time in the history of me and middle school, I could actually be *happy* about something going onto my permanent record.

Go, Falcons, go!

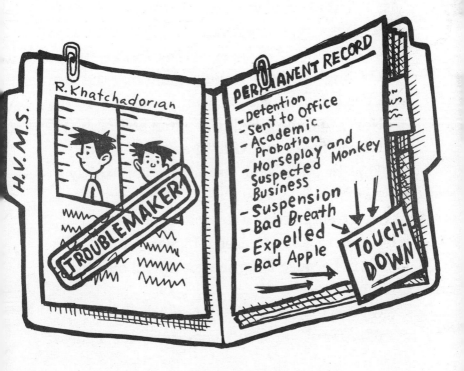

CHAPTER 40

GiRL TROUBLe, ON THe DOUBLe

After the game was over (Southside 38, Hills Village 6), Mom gave me a big hug, and then Grandma gave me one of her freaky-strong HUGE hugs. Seriously, Dotty could hug the skin off a boa constrictor if she wanted to.

"Next stop, the NBA!" Grandma said.

"Do you mean the NFL?" I asked her.

"That too," she said. Grandma's not exactly a sports fan, but at least she's a Rafe fan.

Even Georgia was a tiny bit impressed. "I guess you're going to need a bigger helmet," she told me, "because I can see your head blowing up already."

"We don't wear helmets," I said.

"Whatever," she said. "Congratulations, I guess."

Then Mom said she was taking us all to Swifty's for burgers, including Flip if he wanted, and I told her I'd go find out.

Which I did. But first, I made a quick swing by the snack bar—also known as accidentally-on-purpose-bumping-into-Jeanne-Galletta-after-I'd-scored-a-touchdown. (I mean, seriously, can you blame me?)

Jeanne was just packing up the candy bars and soda cups when I got there.

"Hi, Rafe!" she said. "Great job today!"

"Oh, hi, Jeanne," I said, like I didn't even know she was going to be there. But we could have had ESPN reporters all around us and the president of the United States asking for my autograph, and the only person I would have seen was Jeanne, Jeanne, Jeanne.

"I heard you scored a touchdown," Jeanne said.

"You...heard?" I said.

"We were pretty busy, so I didn't get to see the game," she told me.

"Oh, gotcha," I said, trying to sound like I wasn't totally bummed out now. I'd just had my Big Moment, and Jeanne was too busy putting fake butter on popcorn to notice.

"Well, uh…that's okay. I was just coming over to get a Snickers," I said. Right before—

"Hi, Rafe!" someone else said behind me.

I turned around and Marley Grote was standing there. I'd known Marley since about first grade. She was okay, I guess.

"Hey, Marley," I said.

"You were awesome today!" she said.

"Thanks," I said, but I was still looking at Jeanne.

"How did you know all that running around was going to work?" Marley said. "It was crazy! Mega-crazy!"

I'll bet you anything Marley is someone's little sister. It's like they're all programmed to show up and start talking at exactly the wrong time.

"Sorry, Marley," I said, "but Jeanne and I were kind of having a conversation."

Jeanne looked up like she was thinking, *We were?*

"Oh," Marley said. Then she laughed. I don't know why. "Well, I guess I'll see you in school," she told me, and ran over to where Amy Bernstein was waiting. The two of them started whispering and they walked away like they were attached at the head.

When I looked back at Jeanne again, she didn't seem too happy. In fact, she had her mad-at-Rafe face on. Believe me, I know what that one looks like. I just wasn't sure how I'd blown it this time.

"What?" I said.

"That was so rude," she said.

"It was?"

"Marley obviously likes you—"

"She does?"

"And you just completely blew her off. Nice going."

I didn't know what to say to that. Why did Jeanne think Marley liked me? How could she tell so fast?

And what were the chances of getting a do-over on this one?

Jeanne took a deep breath and shook her head like I was some kind of lost cause. Or like that touchdown didn't mean anything at all.

"I'll see you later, Rafe," she said.

"But…" I said.

"I have to close up," she said.

"But…but…Snickers?" I said. Right before she slammed that snack bar window closed in my face. And on my heart. Again.

I know, I know. I'm pathetic. I have a better chance of throwing a pool party on the sun than I do of getting Jeanne Galletta to fall in love with me. But that doesn't mean I don't still want her to like me, or at least think I'm not a complete jerk. The truth is, Jeanne's been there for me more than once. If she ever needed anything, all she'd have to do is ask.

But unless GO AWAY counted as needing something from me, I didn't think that was going to be happening anytime soon.

Better luck next lifetime.

COOL KiDS' TABLE

Hang on. The good parts of this story aren't over yet. In fact, some of the best stuff is coming up. (And then some of the worst too. It's kind of a roller-coaster ride from here to the end, so hold on tight.)

The next day at school, a lot of people were really nice to me. They were saying stuff like "What a touchdown!" and "Way to go, Khatchadorian." Which was a weird feeling. Usually it was more like "What a dork!" and "Get out of the way, Khatchadorian."

I put up some new art too. It was my drawing of *The Thinker*, but in honor of the Falcons, I added a little extra something this time.

That one went right on the trophy case. And here's a shocker for you: Mrs. Stricker walked right by it and let it stay up for a while. Which made it a pretty good day for SAM *and* for Rafe.

In English, Quinn Richardson told me he was having a party that Saturday at his house. I was pretty sure that meant I was invited, but I wasn't positive.

Then at lunch, I came into the cafeteria, and all the Falcons were eating at the same big table.

"Over here!" Flip said, and waved at me to come sit down.

You know when you think someone's talking to the person behind you, but then you look and nobody's there? It felt like that. Except this was Flip, so I figured it out pretty fast.

"I decided we're going to call that crazy play of yours Khatch and Scatter," Flip told me when I put my tray down. "Khatch, like *Khatch*adorian," he said. "Get it?"

"Yeah, I get it," I told him. "But I couldn't run that play again if I tried." I remembered Miller passing me the ball, and I remembered getting power-mugged in the end zone. But the rest was kind of a blur.

Still, once Flip made up his mind, that was it. So okay, Khatch and Scatter. I liked it, actually. I'd never had a football play named after me.

I'd never sat at a cool kids' table either. It was like visiting a foreign country.

"Yo, Khatchadorian!" Jeremy yelled from the other end of the table. "We've got your MVP trophy over here. Stand by for delivery."

I looked over, and Jeremy was opening a carton of chocolate milk. But he was also smiling in this way that said, *I'm not JUST opening a chocolate milk, so pay attention.* Everyone else was starting to watch too.

"What's going on?" I asked Flip.

"You'll see," he said.

Jeremy opened the milk carton up wide and passed it to Richie Franklin. Richie dropped a Tater Tot inside and passed it on to Calvin Penn. Calvin added a couple spoonfuls of creamed corn and passed it over to Miller. Then Miller ripped open a packet of ketchup.

"Can't have Tater Tots without ketchup," he said, and squirted it in. Then he closed the carton, shook it up, and slid the whole thing over to me.

If Flip hadn't been sitting there cheesing away, I would have thought this was Miller and the guys picking on me, all over again. But something about this felt different. This was more like a dare. The good kind.

"Drink, drink, drink, drink," Flip said, right before the rest of the team started saying it too.

I mean, it's not like I was *excited* about drinking that chocolate-corn-tater milk. But I did kind of like the way they were all looking at me, waiting to see what I'd do.

So you *know* I went for it, right?

The first swallow was the hardest. It tasted like…well, like chocolate, corn, potato, and ketchup. The guys all laughed like crazy when some of the milk spilled right out of the sides of my mouth.

Which made me laugh too.

Which made me spit.

Which made all of us laugh even harder— but not as hard as we did when some of that chocolate milk came dripping out of my nose. There might have been some creamed corn in there too. It was hard to tell. Meanwhile, the guys were yelling my name, and pounding their fists on the table, and it was completely amazing, and totally hilarious…

…right up until Mrs. Stonecase came swooping in for the kill.

"WHAT is the nature of this disturbance?" she said. "And WHO is responsible for this mess?"

Just like that, I knew I was busted. Stonecase looked ready to start slicing and dicing as soon as someone pled guilty, but I was still trying to swallow what was left in my mouth.

And here's where things got even more interesting.

Before I could tell Mrs. Stonecase anything, Flip piped up. "I did it," he said. "It's my mess, Mrs. Stonecase."

"No, it's *my* mess," Jeremy said.

"Actually, it's mine," I said. But everyone kept on going.

"Me too," Miller said.

"Me three," Quinn said.

Within a minute, every Falcon at that table took credit for the whole thing. Mrs. Stonecase thought it was hilarious too, and gave us all the rest of the day off from school.

Yeah, right after she quit her job, little green men landed on the lawn outside, and Jeanne Galletta decided to fall in love with me after all.

"Enough!" Mrs. Stonecase said. "Is there anyone at this table to whom this mess does not belong?"

Nobody made a move.

"Fine," she said. Then she whipped out her phone and took a picture of all of us sitting at that table.

"I will see every one of you in detention, first thing after school on Friday," Stonecase said, looking at the picture. "No getting out of it now."

"Detention?" Quinn said.

"Seriously?" Jeremy said.

"That was smooth," Flip said. "Did you see how she did that?"

"And if this mess isn't cleaned up in five minutes, you can make it three detentions. EACH!" Mrs. Stonecase told us. Then she put the phone back in her pocket like she was holstering a weapon. Which she kind of was.

Friday detention was the worst—as in, the most work. I figured the guys were going to quit fooling around now and throw me right under the bus.

But they didn't. They all just shut up and took it. Even Miller! So now, maybe for the first time ever, the whole Hills Village Middle School football team was going to have one massive detention.

I'm not saying I was looking forward to it. And I'm not saying I was proud of myself. But…it *was* kind of awesome.

Just don't tell my mom I said that.

FANS

Question: How did my mom feel about the detention when I told her?

Answer: How do you think?

She wanted to make me quit football on the spot, but I talked her into a warning instead. One more screwup and I was going to be the world's next former Falcon.

After dinner, Mom told me to go to my room and do my homework. Which I did. But first, I went online and checked my Art-Gunk account. Loozer was up to forty-two fans by now. I also had eighteen new comments waiting for me. And eleven of them were good!

That blew me away. It was like the cherry on the sundae. Or forty-two cherries!

You know what's better than having one secret identity? Having *two* secret identities! It was like my new hobby or something. Now I had R. K. Whatchamacallit online and SAM at school. Which was way better than being plain old Rafe Khatchadorian all the time.

Leo was into it too.

"We're famous!" he said.

"You're famous," I told him. "I'm anonymous."

"Don't worry, I won't forget about you when I'm making movies and millions all at the same time."

"Better not," I told him. "You're going to need me to open a bank account. They only give them to real people."

"Good point," Leo said. "And speaking of good points, was I right about taking it easy, or was I right?"

"You were right," I said. "But does Operation: S.A.M. count as taking it easy?"

"Sure, it's not causing any trouble, and it might even be doing some good. Sometimes you've just got to relax and let the good stuff happen," he said.

I couldn't argue with that. It had been a pretty amazing couple of days.

NEWEST NEWS

Loozer and Leo in: "LOOZER AND LEO: THE MOVIE" BREAKS ALL BOX OFFICE RECORDS!

"The best movie that will ever exist." - EVERYONE

Leo the Silent, the FIRST Imaginary Billionaire.

"The money's real."

"I never thought they'd amount to anything," said former principal Ida P. Stricker.

R.K. Whatchamacallit: WHO IS HE??? Or she? Or we? What we know on PAGE 21

SEQUEL ALREADY IN THE WORKS! "Loozer and Leo: The Movie, Part Two: The Meatloaf Mysteries"

Expected to be a romping, stomping, galloping laugh riot but also a drama and maybe action-packed?

Did Loozer and Leo buy a solid-gold helicopter and an island made of candy??

Our reporter finds the truth! Bubblegum Island is real! Helicopter is just made of silver.

BUT...
BUT...
BUT...

There's one big difference between me and Leo. If things are going well, that's all that matters to him. Leo doesn't have to worry about real-life stuff.

I do. And this is *my* real life we're talking about. I didn't think for a second that everything was just going to keep getting better and better and better to infinity. It doesn't work that way. No matter how good it's going, there's always a Tater Tot somewhere in the chocolate milk, if you know what I mean.

It's just a question of how long it takes to float to the surface.

MAKE A STATEMENT

The next day in art, Ms. Donatello had a new assignment for us.

"I want you to think about making a statement with your art," she said.

"Huh?" Felicia Tollery said. "I don't get it."

I was glad someone else didn't.

"What do you mean, a statement?" I asked. "Like, 'I'm hungry'?" (Art was right before lunch, and I was starving.)

"Not exactly," Ms. D said. "Art isn't just about images. It's also about ideas. It's about saying something to the world. Maybe even changing the world for the better."

Then she showed us some famous examples, so we could see who we *weren't* going to live up to on this one.

The first was a painting called *American Gothic*. I always think that name sounds like there should be vampires in there, or at least people wearing black and listening to weird music. But it's more like the opposite—just some farmer and his wife standing in front of a house. (Ms. D said the house was the gothic part, but I didn't get that either.)

Now, THIS is gothic.

American Gothic, by Grant Wood

"It looks like an ordinary portrait, doesn't it? But the artist, Grant Wood, was also making his own kind of statement," Ms. Donatello said. "It's about the strength and dignity of Americans at a difficult time. These people represent survivors."

This was the kind of thing we talked about in real art school, when I went to Cathedral and Airbrook. Ms. D kept saying she wanted us to think BIG, and I guess you don't get much bigger than changing the world.

The question was—how? What was my statement going to be? And why would anyone care, anyway?

When I looked up again, there was another slide on the screen. It was a creepy-looking black-and-white painting.

"What did Pablo Picasso have in mind here?" Ms. Donatello asked. "What statement do you think *Guernica* is making?"

And I thought, *Good question.*

But then I started to see it. There were faces, and people kind of hidden in that painting. Some of them looked like they were screaming, and some were more like ghosts.

Guernica, by Pablo Picasso

"They don't look too happy," I said.

"No. They're not," Ms. Donatello said. "This painting is about war. Picasso was using his artistic genius to speak out about events in the Spanish Civil War of 1937.

"So you see, a statement can be quiet, like *American Gothic*. Or it can be loud and forceful, like the images in *Guernica*," Ms. D said. "It can also be just as straightforward as this."

← <u>Love</u>, by
Robert Indiana

"That's kind of goofy," Ava Bartlett said.

"It's also a classic piece of art," Ms. D said. "And nobody can mistake Mr. Indiana's message here, am I right?"

She showed us some other examples after that, but I already had plenty to think about with this one. Like what my "statement" was supposed to be. And how to say something that was going to "change the world." And maybe most important of all—what to have for lunch.

Because who can think about changing the world on an empty stomach?

CHAPTER 44

TALKING IN CODE

When I was on my way out of the art room, Ms. D asked me if I had a minute to "talk."

"Okay," I said. But I thought, *Uh-oh! Where is this headed?*

"Do you have any ideas for your statement piece?" she asked me.

"I don't know," I told her. "It's a big assignment."

"Don't think about it too much," she said. "Sometimes it's very simple. For instance, I think even this 'SAM' fellow is making a statement with his art."

"You do?" I said. And I thought, *UH-OH! I think I know where this is headed.*

"I think he's saying 'Art is worth looking at,'" Ms. D said. "But what do *you* think, Rafe?"

And I thought, *RED ALERT! RED ALERT! WE ARE DEFINITELY UNDER ATTACK!*

"Rafe?" Ms. D said, waving a hand in front of my eyes. "Hello? Anyone there?"

"Huh?" I said. "Sorry, what?"

"I was saying that a person can learn a lot from copying the masters like that," Ms. Donatello told me. "But it's good to do your own thing too. I just hope 'SAM' understands that. Whoever he is."

By now, I was about 99.9 percent sure that Ms. Donatello was talking in code, like she was giving me a message. I wasn't going to confess about my two secret identities—they're called secret for a reason. But it was pretty obvious she didn't need me to.

But she didn't seem mad. The more I stood there, the more it felt like maybe this wasn't a red alert. More like orange. Or yellow. Or maybe a green light.

"Keep setting those sights high, Rafe," she told me. "Maybe do something a little different for this new assignment. Something nobody's ever seen before. Do you understand what I'm saying?"

"Yeah," I said. "I think so." Because I'm pretty sure that I finally did.

Ms. Donatello was a good teacher. No—not even that. She was a *great* teacher. The best.

That's what I understood.

CHAPTER 45

AFTER-SCHOOL SPECIAL

That Friday, I was feeling pretty good. I'd done a picture of this painting called *Arrangement in Grey and Black, No.1* and put it on one of the school bulletin boards during second period. The Vacu-Stricker 2000 didn't even make it disappear until sometime during sixth.

Then school was over. Usually, hearing the dismissal bell on a Friday makes me happier than Junior in a hot dog factory.

But *this* Friday, the bell might as well have been an emergency alarm. I could have used a warning about the torture that was about to start, thanks to a one-two combo punch of torture from Mrs. Stonecase and Coach Shumsky.

It started with our full-team detention. Mrs.

Stonecase gave us a whole lecture to get things rolling. She said this was punishment for our "deplorable, pernicious, yet predictable stunt in the cafeteria." I don't know what *pernicious* means, but I'm pretty sure it's not about being awesome and hilarious with chocolate milk.

After that, she put us to work. She divided us up and got us washing desks, sweeping the bathrooms, mopping the halls, and organizing the supply closets in the office. The whole thing was about a zero on the fun scale, except for five minutes there when Flip got creative with the school's tape supply.

And it wasn't over yet. As soon as we got out of there, Coach Shumsky was waiting for us. He wasn't too happy about the whole team getting in trouble, so he made us stay late for a full football practice on top of detention. He even threw in a little extra suffering for good measure.

And by a little extra suffering, I mean A LOT OF SUFFERING, of course.

We started off with our usual one-mile warm-up. Then we had to do a truckload of wind sprints, a boatload of drills, and a full scrimmage after that.

Plus, the whole time, Coach kept telling us about what it meant to be "good representatives" of the school, "on and off the field."

"Football isn't just a sport," he yelled at us. "It's a way of life!"

"Yeah, and a way of death too," Flip said, right before we stumbled through our hundred and forty-eighth wind sprint.

"If that doesn't mean anything to you, it should," Coach kept going. "You boys need to carry the Falcon name with pride, do you hear me? I said… DO YOU HEAR ME?"

I heard him, I heard him. But right then, it was either run or talk. He couldn't have both.

The good news was, we had another game coming up, and everyone thought we had a decent shot at winning. It was against the Belleville Middle School Raiders. Coach said he was going to make sure we were in "peak form" by the time the Raiders rolled into town. But I'm pretty sure that was just code for "Detention Part Two."

Still, even though I'd rather have been anywhere else in the world than on that field right then, some little part of me was getting excited about that game. I'd gotten a taste of being good at something that I never in a million years thought I'd be good at, and I wanted more. Maybe I'd get to score another touchdown… or two…or three. And maybe Jeanne would get to see it happen this time. Then the Falcons would get on a roll. We'd just keep winning and winning…and winning…until we were state champions. No, WORLD CHAMPIONS! And if I played it right and got really lucky, it could all be thanks to me! So when I got up there to accept my Heisman Middle School Trophy at the internationally televised World Sports Banquet,

I'd look right into those cameras, I'd smile wide, and I'd say—

"THIS ISN'T A PLAYDATE, KHATCHA-DORIAN! PICK UP THOSE KNEES AND KEEP UP! DON'T SLOW DOWN NOW, BECAUSE WE'RE JUST GETTING STARTED HERE!"

If Coach Shumsky didn't kill me first.

Sorry, Coach, I won't be at practice tomorrow.

CHAPTER 46

PARTY DOWN

The good news was, I had a whole weekend to recover from that mega-practice. Not only that, but Quinn's team party was Saturday night. There were going to be hot dogs and soda, movies in the basement, and a huge ice cream cake in the shape of a football.

At least, that's what I told Mom, because that's what Quinn told me.

I went with Flip. When we got to Quinn's house, I could hear music coming from the basement, but the whole upstairs seemed kind of empty. I didn't see his mom and dad anywhere.

"Come on down," Quinn said. "Everyone's here."

"Where are your parents?" I asked him.

"Exactly," he said.

Which started to tell me what kind of party this *actually* was.

I'd never been to a real middle school party before. Not unless you count that one lame dance at summer camp—and you shouldn't. So I was actually kind of nervous and excited on my way down those stairs.

Well, more nervous than excited.

Okay…just nervous.

In the basement, there weren't too many lights on. The music was up loud and a bunch of people were dancing in a big clump. I saw some guy-shaped shadows and some girl-shaped shadows, but it was too dark to tell who anyone was.

Quinn told us there were some chips and stuff, so we went for those first. He even had a bunch of cold Zoom, which is my favorite drink.

"Hey, Flip," I said, "you want some of this?" But when I turned around, there was just an empty space where Flip used to be. You know how good he is at keeping still, right? He was already out there dancing with everyone, like there was nothing to it.

The thing is, I'm about as good at dancing as I am at talking to girls. One-legged ostriches have better dance moves than I have.

Which left me standing by the chip bowl on my own, like a giant flashing LOSER sign.

Basically, I'd been at Quinn's house for about eighty-two seconds, and I was starting to wonder why I ever thought this party was a good idea. As far as I could tell, there were about fifteen people having a great time, and then there was me. I felt as popular as a cactus.

So after a while, I headed for the nearest corner and sat down on one of the couches in the dark. I know when I'm better off sticking to the sidelines. Not that I had much of a choice.

"Hey," someone said.

I looked over and there was a girl sitting at the other end of the couch. I hadn't even seen her there in the dark. I didn't recognize her, but she was pretty. Which made me instantly nervous, of course.

"Hey," I said.

"I'm Page," she said. "I'm Carissa's cousin, visiting from out of town."

"Hi, I'm Rafe," I said—but my voice decided to crack just then, so it sounded like there was a duck living right in the middle of my name.

Great.

Just great.

The music stopped suddenly, right in the middle of a song. I was super-grateful because Page looked away to see what was going on.

"Okay, boys and girls," Quinn said loudly. "Time for a little game!"

Finally, something fun to do! I thought about telling everyone how to play baconball, but I didn't know if Quinn had a dog. Or bacon. Or a ball. So I kept my mouth shut.

Good thing too, because baconball wasn't exactly the kind of game he was talking about.

Quinn held up an empty water bottle and grinned. One by one, all the other kids started smiling too, like they were in on a joke I didn't get. Even Flip.

I looked over at Page and she winked.

"What's that for?" I whispered.

"You'll see," she whispered back, then got up and reached out her hand. She pulled me off the couch and onto the carpet, where everyone was sitting in a big circle.

Oh no.

Still grinning, Quinn put the bottle in the middle of the circle.

No no no.

Then he looked right at me. "As the Most Valuable Player in the game, Rafe gets the first spin!"

NOOOOOO!!!!

CHAPTER 47

THE RUNAWAY

Since boy-girl parties were a brand-new thing for me, I'd never played Spin the Bottle before, but I did know that it usually involved—well—spinning a bottle.

And kissing the person it's pointing to.

Don't get me wrong. The idea of kissing a girl was fine. The idea of kissing a girl I might not even know or like while all the cool kids in school were watching?

But like with all the un-fun stuff in my life, I didn't have a choice. I shuffled over to the middle of the circle, knelt down, and grabbed the bottle. I closed my eyes and spun it before I could even let

NOT FINE!

myself think about who I did or didn't want it to land on.

Because I had to keep being the person everyone wanted me to be. The MVP. The cool kid with all the right moves.

I opened my eyes when all the whistles and claps started ripping through the room. The bottle was pointing at someone...a girl.

Page.

You'd think I'd be relieved to kiss a pretty girl like Page, but I wasn't. Not by a long shot. Just the thought got me sweating in places I'd never sweated before. Even my earlobes were getting drippy.

Oh, man...oh, man...oh, man! This was supposed to be a good thing, right? I'd been wishing for a pretty girl to kiss me since about day one of middle school. And now it was happening. My first real kiss.

So then, if this was such a good thing, why was I so...freaking...SCARED?

Sometimes my life is unbelievably confusing. On the one hand, I just wanted to be smooth Rafe and kiss her and have fun like everyone else.

On the other hand, I was feeling about ready to barf all over her shoes.

"Hello? Rafe?" Page asked. She smiled.

Which, I reminded myself, meant that she was not totally disgusted by the idea of a kiss from me.

I turned to face her and she closed her eyes. But I could feel a zillion other laser eyes on me.

I leaned in.

And then I froze.

I couldn't do it.

Not like this.

After a few decades went by, Page opened her eyes again. She looked confused. I know I had a dumb, deer-in-the-headlights look on my face, which probably didn't make her any less confused.

I thought—*SAY SOMETHING, RAFE! SOMETHING FUNNY. SOMETHING SMOOTH. ANYTHING!*

JUST…OPEN YOUR STUPID MOUTH AND SAY SOMETHING RIGHT NOW!

"Um…I have to go to the bathroom," I said, and a wave of giggles and chortles zipped right around the circle of kids staring at me.

"Um...okay," Page said. Now she was kind of looking at me like I was starting to grow an extra limb.

"I'll be right back," I told her. Even though it was totally possible at that point that she was hoping I *wouldn't* be back.

Everyone was still staring and cackling as I slowly backed out of the Circle of Agony. I couldn't look Page in the face, or anyone else. Flip was nowhere to be seen—he was probably upstairs raiding the refrigerator and had missed the whole thing.

I wish I'd missed it too. Raiding the refrigerator with Flip sounded like heaven right about now.

As I scrambled up the basement stairs, every good feeling from my touchdown and being on the team melted away like a snowman in the Sahara. I heard laughter and squeals behind me as someone else spun the bottle and did what they were supposed to do.

So why couldn't I?

I swerved away from the hallway where the bathroom was, opened the front door, and walked out without once looking back.

Right before I started running.

CHAPTER 48

DÉJÀ POO

"**T**hat was fast," Mom said when I came into the house. She and Grandma and Georgia were on the couch watching *The Princess Bride*, even though they've all seen it about a hundred times. "Did you forget something?"

"No, I just, um…I mean, yeah. I forgot to walk Junior," I said.

"No, you didn't," Georgia said. "You walked him right after dinner."

"Well, as long as I'm here…" I said. "Here, boy!"

I couldn't even think about answering any questions right now. So I clipped on Junior's leash. A few seconds later, I was on my way back out the door.

"Rafe?" Mom said.

When I looked at her, I could tell she knew something was up. Mom's psychic, in that typical Mom kind of way. But she didn't make a big deal out of it.

"Just around the block, okay?" she said.

I told her that was no problem and headed out.

Somewhere along the way, I stopped watching where I was going and Junior took over. When I looked up again, we were almost all the way to his favorite place on earth—the dog park. You can always tell you're getting close because he starts pulling on the leash like he's going to die if we get there a second later than we have to.

I figured it couldn't hurt to make a quick stop. It wasn't *that* late, and it looked like there were still a lot of people out with their dogs.

Then my mind just started cranking, and not with happy smiley thoughts.

Mostly, I wished I'd never gotten invited to Quinn's party. It was like my whole life had turned into a game of Chutes and Ladders. Just when things were heading up, up, up, I had to go and land on a big fat slide, all the way back to the bottom.

Once we were inside the fence, Junior got right to it, saying hi to all his friends and sniffing a few new butts around the park. But then, pretty quick, he started walking in little circles—right before he went into that old familiar squat.

And that's when I remembered something. You always, always want to bring a plastic bag to the dog park with you.

"Isn't that your dog?" some lady said.

"Yeah," I said. "You don't have an extra bag, do you?"

She just made a face like I was totally useless. "Are you kidding me?" she said.

"I forgot."

"Everyone's responsible for their messes, kid. That's how it works," she said. "If you can't look after your own dog—"

"I know, I know," I said, and started walking over to where Junior had done his business. I didn't want to get yelled at anymore. *Maybe I could use one of my socks*, I thought. But then—

"Hey, do you need a bag?" someone behind me asked.

When I turned around, Marley Grote was standing there looking at me. It was like déjà vu from the day of the football game. Except this time, instead of scoring a touchdown, I was picking up poop. Besides that, it was exactly the same.

"Here," she said. She had a little plastic dog bone on her leash, with a whole roll of bags inside.

"You come prepared," I said.

"Like I have a choice, with my dad," she said, and pointed at some guy over on a park bench, feeding a baby. "Why aren't you at Quinn's party?" she asked.

"Well, I was," I said. "But…Junior needed a walk."

"Oh," she said.

"Why aren't *you* at Quinn's party?" I said.

Marley looked at me kind of funny. "I wasn't invited," she told me.

That's when I figured out I shouldn't have asked in the first place. Oops…again.

"You didn't miss much," I said. *Except for the single most humiliating moment of my life.* "Hey, sorry if I was rude or whatever at the game the other day."

"You weren't rude," she said.

"Jeanne thought I was," I told her. "But I didn't mean to be."

Marley smiled, and kind of blushed. I think that was her way of saying, *Yeah, okay, you were a jerk, but I'm not going to make a big deal about it.* Which was pretty nice, I thought. I didn't think I could sink any lower anyway.

"Which dog is yours?" I asked her.

She pointed over to a tree where three little dogs were all sniffing the same spot.

"The white one with the pink collar," she said.

"What's her name?" I said.

"Justine Bieber," she said.

"Seriously?" I said.

"Yeah, why?"

"No reason," I said, because I'd already been rude once, or maybe even twice. I didn't want to push my luck.

Besides, it looked like Junior was starting to make eyes at Justine. So who was I to get in the way?

Maybe at least one of us could have a good night after all.

FALCONS AND SPECIALS

Monday morning, I totally expected everyone to give me a hard time about what happened at the party. I even tried faking sick so I wouldn't have to go to school, but Mom knew a hot washcloth to the face when she saw one.

The one person I told anything to—and I'd already told him everything—was Flip. I said I wasn't really into the game, which was true. He was totally cool about it. Which I knew he would be. Which is why Flip is awesome.

Once I got to school, I spent the whole morning waiting for someone to tell me how lame I was or make kissy noises or whatever else. But nobody said a single word.

At first that seemed like a good thing. But then

I started to wonder. Did anyone even *notice* I'd left the party? Anyone besides Flip, I mean? Probably not.

Not that I wanted them to.

Right?

Then I passed Page's cousin Carissa in the hall and she turned away like she didn't see me. Maybe she thought I didn't kiss Page because I didn't like her. Which wasn't true. How could I not like someone I didn't even know?

I couldn't help being kind of jumpy all the way through Learning Skills. Miller was sitting out there at his usual computer the whole time, surfing away. I figured if anyone was going to get on my case about the party, it would be him. I know we still had our little deal going on, but this was *Miller the Killer* we were talking about. And I still didn't trust him.

So when the period was over and Miller just let me walk by without saying anything, I'll admit it—I was pretty glad. Maybe that whole party disaster was just going to fade off into the sunset and I'd never have to hear about it again.

In fact, I was about halfway through a big sigh of relief, when I heard a familiar sound.

SKREECH!

It was someone pushing their chair back from one of the computers. And then I heard Miller's voice.

"What's up, dweebs?" he said.

I hung back in the library door, just out of sight, and peeked around the corner. Miller was sitting there, blocking Jonny and Maya's way out. Tug was there too, watching and grinning like a second-baboon-in-command.

"Excuse us!" Maya said, all friendly like she usually was.

"What's that class in there?" Miller said.

And I thought—seriously? Couldn't he at least get some new material?

"It's Learning Skills," Jonny said. "It's for kids who need extra help."

For some reason that cracked Miller and Tug up. The thing about Jonny is, he's great at reading books, but not so much with people. He doesn't always know when someone's making a joke. Including one about him.

"What do they call you in there?" Miller said. "Factoid?"

"That's right," Jonny said.

"Okay, so tell us something we don't know," Tug said. "And then we'll let you guys go."

"Why are you being like this?" Maya said.

"Like what?" Miller asked her, all innocent. "We just want Factoid here to show us what he knows."

"Well, for instance, the world's biggest crocodile

and the world's smallest man are from the same island in the Philippines," Jonny said.

"See that?" Tug said. "That wasn't so hard. Tell us something else."

Then Maya spoke up. "Mrs. Seagrave! These boys are bothering us!"

"QUIET!" Mrs. Seagrave yelled, because she's so sweet and cuddly that way. But it was enough to break things up, anyway.

"Come on, Jonny," Maya said, and they kind of squeezed by Miller and Tug. Except just when Jonny walked past, Tug knocked his books out of his hands and they all fell on the floor.

"Careful there, Factoid," Tug said. "You keep dropping stuff, you're going to lose something."

Now Miller was the one cracking up. And I was the one standing there watching, and knowing I should do something, but not doing anything.

It felt kind of complicated. I was on Miller and Tug's team, technically. We were all Falcons and all that. But I was also sort of on Maya and Jonny's team—the Specials. I just wished that meant something besides what it actually meant.

I wished it a lot.

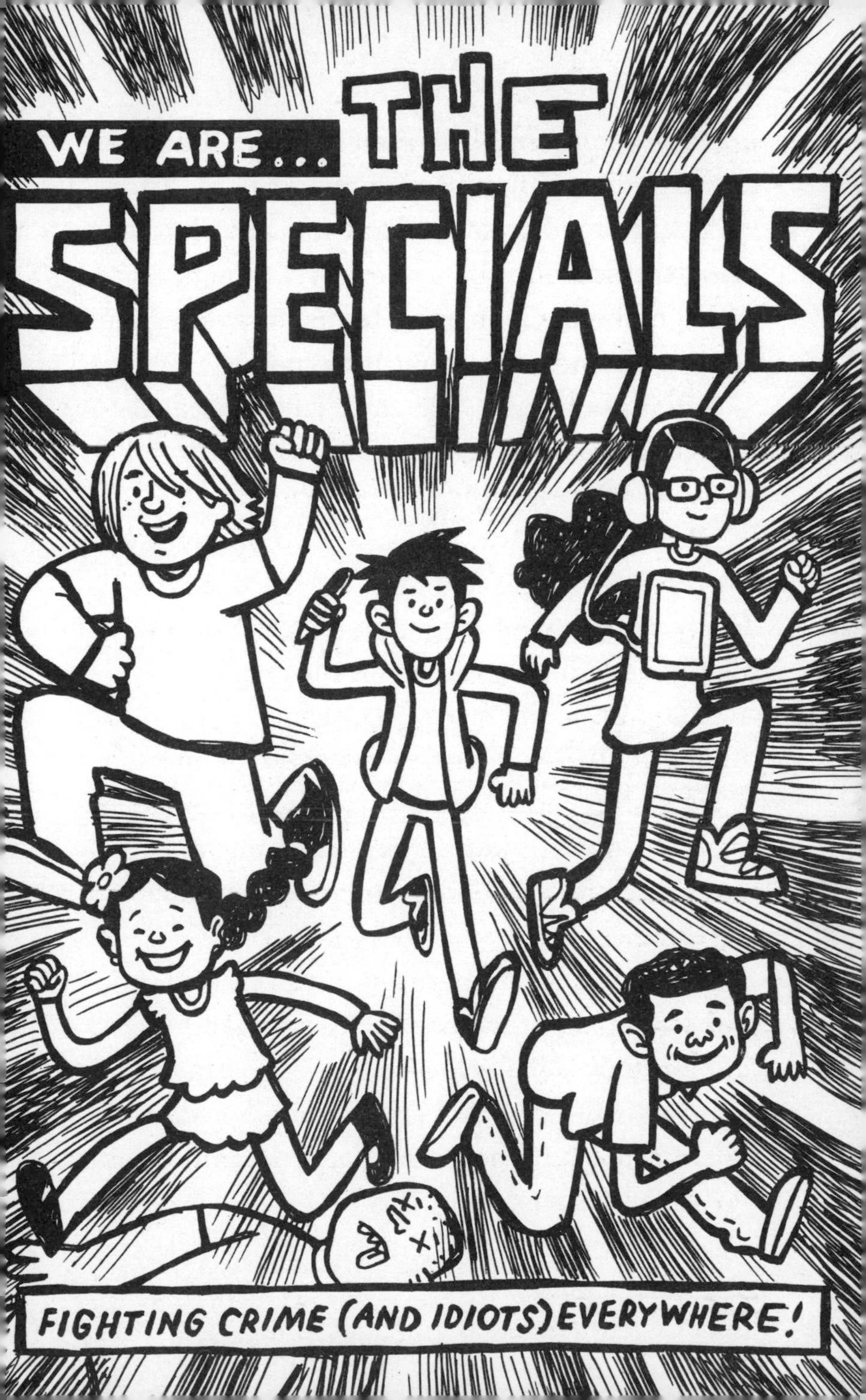
WE ARE... THE SPECIALS
FIGHTING CRIME (AND IDIOTS) EVERYWHERE!

And even though I knew it was wrong to turn around and walk away, that's what I did. After what happened at the party, I couldn't risk being the school bull's-eye again. I thought it would make me feel better to just keep my head down and not worry about it too much.

But guess what?

It didn't.

CHAPTER 50

IT'S NEVER TOO LATE

I guess I could have talked to Flip about all this. Or Mom. Or even Mr. Fanucci. But I didn't. To tell the truth, I didn't want to admit to anyone that I'd walked away like that.

At least, I didn't want to admit it to anyone real. So that night, I talked it over with Leo instead.

"I should have said something," I told him. "If it weren't for football, Miller would be torturing *me*, not them. And now I feel like a jerk all over again. It's like there's no right answer anymore."

As usual, Leo was pretty good about making me feel better. Not only that, but he always has an awesome idea or two up his imaginary sleeve.

"You know, it's not too late," he said.

"Too late for what?" I said.

"To *say* something," he told me.

"What do you mean?"

"You know what I mean," he said. "Just think about it."

So I did. And that's when the million little lightbulbs started going on. It was also when I started figuring out what I wanted to do for Ms. Donatello's assignment.

The more Leo and I talked about it, the better it got. Ms. D wanted me to make a statement? Do my own original artwork? Set my sights high?

Done, done, and done.

But I was still going to keep it a secret, and I was still going to put it up where everyone could see it. Not only that, but this time it was going to go somewhere that Mrs. Stricker wouldn't be able to take it down, no matter how hard she tried.

It was time to take Operation: S.A.M. to a whole new level.

CHAPTER 51

SECRET ARTIST MAN 2.0

By the next morning, I was all fired up and ready to start.

First, I asked Grandma if I could borrow her phone for the day. Mom always needs hers, but Grandma's mostly just sits on her dresser. When she asked me what it was for, I told her it was an art project, which was 100 percent true. And that was good enough for Dotty.

Before I left for school, I went into my room and practiced my moves a little bit. I put Junior on the bed and took some pictures of him with Grandma's phone. But I held the phone down by my side so it didn't *look* like I was taking pictures. At least half of them came out off-center, or blurry, or both. But that was actually okay with me. I even kind of liked them better that way, so

you weren't totally sure what you were looking
at. It felt more like art.

Then I tucked Grandma's phone in my backpack, kissed Mom good-bye, and headed out for
my big day.

It turned out it wasn't so hard to get pictures
of the stuff I wanted. All I had to do was keep
my eyes open, especially when there weren't
any teachers around. Like in the hall, in the
bathroom, in the locker room, on the bus, outside
the school, and on the stairs.

I got my first few shots on the bus, when
Jeremy Savin was neck-clamping a kid and
pushing him out of the backseat.

Then just before first period, I saw some guys trying to shove Alvin Wu into his locker. Caught that too!

In third period, when we were supposed to be reading silently, Felicia Tollery and Ava Barlett were making fun of Dee-Dee's iPad and pointing at her behind her back.

And the whole time, SAM was right there to catch all of it.

Then at lunch, I was about to snap a picture of some sixth graders getting kicked off their table by some eighth graders, when I heard a familiar voice behind me.

"What exactly do you think you're doing, Mr. Khatchadorian?"

"I, um…just wanted to make a call," I said, holding up Grandma's phone.

"Cell phone use is *not* allowed during the school day without permission," she said.

"I know. But it was kind of an emergency."

"Excuse me, but there is no such thing as 'kind of an emergency,'" she said—just before Flip fell down and started howling right there on the cafeteria floor.

"OWWWWW! I think I broke my ankle!" he said. "Ow-ow-OWWWWW!"

Flip didn't even know what I was doing. He just saw me getting in hot water and jumped to it. I don't think he even realized he was clutching his belly right after he'd started yelling about his ankle, but it got Mrs. Stricker's attention, anyway. Just long enough for me to disappear. (Thanks, Flip!)

Now all I had to do was stay off Mrs. Stricker's radar until the end of the day, and then I'd be all set.

With Phase One, anyway.

PHASE TWO

Phase Two was all about making art.

When I got home, I had a hundred and three pictures on Grandma's phone. Most of them were garbage shots, but eleven weren't bad, and eight of those were good enough to use.

Mom says that's how art works: "Throw a bunch of stuff at the wall and see what sticks." I guess that means eight of them were sticking. So I loaded those onto the computer and used the painting tool to do my thing.

First, I colored in the people so they were just silhouettes. I used red for the bullies and green for the kids they were messing with. That way you couldn't tell who anyone was, but you could still see what was going on.

I put some more "statement" in there too. Ms. Donatello had asked us to think about what our art was going to say to the world, and my idea was short and sweet: *Be nice.* In fact, I made it even shorter than that.

Once I finished my pictures, I posted them on their own page at Art-Gunk.com. I made a whole separate account for this, so it wouldn't have anything to do with my Loozer comics or R. K. Whatchamacallit. This was supposed to be a stealthy-anonymous, Secret Artist Man thing.

The complicated part was, I couldn't be stealthy-anonymous *and* get credit for the art. But by now, this whole thing was like a car running downhill with no brakes. I couldn't stop it if I wanted to. I'd figure out the Donatello stuff later.

I wasn't done yet either. The pictures on Art-Gunk were my "statement piece," but I still needed people to know where to find them. I mean, what good is a statement if nobody's listening? That's what Phase Three was all about.

And I had a plan for that too.

The next day was game day, and I mean that in two ways. After school, it was going to be the HVMS Falcons against the Belleville Raiders. But it was also game time for *me*. There was going to be a big pep rally in the gym, right after lunch. That was when I had to be ready.

All I needed in the meantime was a bunch of notebook paper, a big fat marker, a glue stick, a little bit of luck, and a few stealthy moves at school, just before the pep rally.

No problem. SAM 2.0 was on the case.

HiDiNG iN PLAiN SiGHT

I am SAM, and this is my latest mission.
This one's like a cross between a house of
cards and a hand grenade with a missing pin. One
wrong move, and—*BOOM!* The whole thing comes
down. I've got to be in a dozen different places at
just the right time, and in just the right order.

Not only that, but this high-tech fortress
disguised as a middle school is crawling with
guards in the middle of the day. The trick is to
act natural when anyone's looking, and then
move like the wind when they're not.

So I walk casually up the corridor, like I belong
here. Deputy Marshal Stonecase passes me by and
I give her a friendly (but not too friendly) nod. She
has no idea I'm working undercover. That's what

the street clothes and prosthetics are for.

As soon as I find myself alone, I swing into action.

First I check my scanners, perfectly camouflaged inside an ordinary-looking backpack. Once they give me the all clear, I continue to the gymnasium.

My first stop is the so-called equipment room. I know it's a flimsy cover for Sergeant Stricker's missile silo, but I can't worry about that now.

I work fast. I work carefully. I try not to think about the pair of fully armed heat-seeking missiles just under the floor. And the millisecond my package is delivered, I move on.

This next maneuver is what you call a speed round. I cruise through the building like a ninja-tornado, dropping tiny subpackages of coded instructions in every empty corner I can locate. Once the inmates start finding them—and they *will* find them—they'll know what to do.

That's it. Within twenty minutes, my mission is complete. The rest of this operation is out of my hands. So I go back to undercover mode and continue my day like none of this ever happened.

In fact, none of it did. (You've got my back, right?) SAM out!

CHAPTER 54

THE BiG REVEAL

By the time Mrs. Stricker got on the intercom
and started telling everyone to go to the gym
for the pep rally, I was sweating like crazy. All
that last-minute running around had me worn
out. But I was ready for Phase Three.

So here's how the pep rally was supposed to go.

While everyone else came into the gym and sat
on the bleachers, the football team would wait in
the locker room.

Then Coach Shumsky would say something
to the crowd. Then some kids from the student
council would bring out this big rolled-up sign
from the equipment room. The cheerleaders
would start cheering, the student council kids
would unroll the sign in front of everyone, and
the sign would say GO, FALCONS, GO! After that, the

team would come running out and bust through it while the whole school watched.

Got it? That's how it was *supposed* to go. And most of it did happen that way, right up to the part about the sign saying GO, FALCONS, GO!

Because that's not all it said.

Not anymore.

So there I was in the locker room, lined up with the team and waiting to go. Coach was giving his pep talk to the crowd, and I was starting to wonder if I'd made any mistakes. What if something went wrong?

"You okay?" Flip said. "You're sweating like a pig. Actually, I don't even know if pigs sweat, but you sure are."

"I'm good," I said. I kind of wished I'd told him about this, but the less Flip knew, the better. For his own sake, anyway.

Besides, it was too late now.

"So without further delay..." Coach Shumsky said. I could hear the sound of that big paper sign starting to unroll (*crinkle, crinkle, crinkle, crinkle*).

"I present to you—"

(*Crinkle, crinkle, crinkle...*)

"The HVMS FALCONS!" Coach said, just before the cheerleaders and everyone else started screaming—

"LET'S GO, FALCONS, LET'S GO!"

Then we all went running out of the locker room. I couldn't see the front of the sign, but I could see everyone on the bleachers, looking back at us. Which is about when the cheering changed from—

to something more like—

Because this is what everyone was seeing:

Meanwhile, all the Falcons at the front of the line went tearing through that sign like it was made out of Belleville Raiders. The rest of us came running behind. By the time we were all standing in front of the school, the whole thing was in a million little shreds on the gym floor.

Mrs. Stricker was looking at Mrs. Stonecase. Mrs. Stonecase was starting to tap on her phone. The cheerleaders were still cheering, and the pep rally was still going on—mostly. But I could see a bunch of kids looking at each other like they were thinking, *What's on that website?*

And I know what you're probably thinking too. What good was that huge sign if it was only in front of everyone for about ten seconds?

But Phase Three wasn't over yet.

And I'm just saying, if everyone started finding little slips of paper after the pep rally—like in their lockers, and the bathrooms, and the library, and the music room—and if those little slips of paper just happened to say the same thing as that sign?

Well, that might have had something to do with me too.

CHAPTER 55

AWESOME AND ANONYMOUS

The rest of the school day was cray-cray-crazy. My whole BNICE thing started spreading faster than a fire in a match factory.

Every time I went by the library, people were looking at those pictures of mine on Art-Gunk. com. And I went by the library a *lot*. I've never gotten so many hall passes in my life.

I could hear people talking about it everywhere too. More than any of my other SAM stuff. One girl had even printed out a picture and taped it on the front of her folder. Which was like free advertising.

Which was awesome. I had definitely made a statement with my art, like Ms. Donatello said I should. It wasn't like anything I'd done for Operation: S.A.M., which was kind of the point.

I wondered if she'd seen any of this yet. And I wondered what she thought.

She'd probably like it, I figured. She might even have been proud of me. Maybe I'd get an A+.

You know...if I could ever figure out a way to tell her I'd done it.

CHAPTER 56

GAME TIME

My day wasn't over yet either. Not by a long shot. You haven't forgotten about the big game against the Belleville Raiders, have you?

By the time we were jogging onto the field for warm-ups that afternoon, I was feeling pretty good. Everything with BNICE had gone even better and bigger than I'd hoped.

And speaking of big, the crowd at this game was about twice the size as at the last game. And even though all those people weren't there just to see *me*, it was fun to pretend they were. For a minute, anway. It felt like *everyone* was there. Mr. Fanucci was sitting with Mom, Grandma, and Georgia, which was weird. Jeanne was working the snack bar again, and hopefully watching more than the popcorn this time. Marley and her friends were sitting at the top of the bleachers with their heads all stuck together like usual.

I thought Coach might put me in the starting lineup this time, but he didn't. For the whole first quarter, I just sat there leaving a Rafe-shaped butt mark on the team bench.

But finally, after the first play of the second quarter, the Falcons took possession and Coach yelled at me to get ready with the rest of the offensive squad.

Part of me got excited, because I wanted to score another touchdown. Or two. Or ten. But part of me was also shaking in my cleats, because I didn't know if I could.

Either way, I wanted to find out.

When we got into the huddle, Tug laid out the play for us. I was so busy trying to focus, I forgot to listen to everything he said. I just heard, "Blah blah blah blah blah blah, and KHATCHADORIAN, you cut up the middle."

At least I got my part, anyway. So I took my place on the line and got ready to go.

As soon as Tug took the snap, one of the Belleville

guys came right for me. I scrambled like a human egg and managed to get past him somehow.

After that, I took a fast run downfield and turned around. Tug saw I was open and got off a nice spiral pass, headed right for me.

I saw the ball...

kept my eye on the ball...

reached up to catch the ball...

and—*WHIFF!*—watched the ball go right through my hands, just before it landed on the field like football roadkill.

Hello, embarrassing.

"All right, all right!" Coach yelled from the sidelines. "We've got this, guys! Just focus and try again!"

It took a few more plays before I got my next chance. This time I was more determined than ever.

I was supposed to go wide, and I did. I got clear of the Belleville defenders, maybe because they weren't taking me too seriously anymore. Either way, I put up my hands, Tug sent another special delivery my way, and—

WHIFF!

I didn't even get a piece of it this time.

Which stunk. Miller was starting to look at me like I was a walking waste of space. And I was starting to wonder if my first-ever touchdown had also been my last-ever touchdown.

It wasn't looking good. At this rate, I was going to be moving back to Miller the Killerville sooner than later. Like maybe right after the game.

Except then something completely unexpected happened. I got a lucky break—and that's not even the most unexpected part.

Because this time, it came from Miller himself.

RUN FOR YOUR LIFE

"Here's what we're going to do," Miller said as soon as we were huddled up for the next play. "Tug, you're going to take the snap. Then you're going to hand off to Khatchadorian. After that, the rest of us are going to make like a road crew and give him an open lane."

Michael Alvarez looked as confused as I was. For one thing, Miller wasn't playing quarterback. But I guess he *was* playing head mouth in charge.

"But Coach said—"

"I know what I'm doing," Miller said. "So listen up. Khatchadorian couldn't catch a cold if someone threw it at him—"

"Um, thanks?" I said.

"But he can run. Can't you, Khatchadorian?" Miller asked me.

"Sure," I said, because that was the only right answer.

"So do that," Miller said. "You get handed the ball, and you run like your life depends on it, because it does. I want to win this thing. Anyone got a problem with that?"

I guess nobody did, because a second later, we were lining up the play.

Quinn snapped Tug the ball. Tug dropped back. I cut around and took the hand-off from him, just like Miller said. Then, while everyone else was blocking like crazy, I started running like crazy.

"GO!" Miller said.

So I went. It was like I was on fire, and not in a good way. Or maybe it *was* good, since it got me running downfield as fast as I've ever run. I just kept thinking about Miller coming after me with that Rafe-eating look in his eye, and that pretty much did the trick. The next thing I knew, I was running for my life right into the end zone.

Touchdown! Falcons score!

Khatchadorian lives to see another day!

People were yelling, and the team was all over me again, and I could hear my mom screaming louder than anybody else in the stands.

"WAY TO GO, SWEETIE!"

I could have done without that "sweetie," but I'm not going to get picky. It was all awesomely, awesomely awesome.

And get this. Are you ready? Coach was all over it. He didn't yell at Miller for calling the play, or anything. In fact, at halftime he said we were going to try it again and see what happened.

Long story short, Miller's idea worked two more times. That's how long it took Belleville to figure it out and start covering me like poison ivy.

But by then it was too late for them. Final score: Falcons 25, Raiders 18. And I'd run for three—count 'em, *three!*—touchdowns. I didn't know if that was any kind of school record at HVMS, but it was definitely a world record on Planet Rafe.

I felt like I was in some kind of movie, starring someone else. Anyone but me.

Except...it WAS me.

And in the weirdest possible way, it was all thanks to Miller.

CHAPTER 58

LiKe TALKiNG TO A
BRiCK WALL

After I got hugged by Mom, crushed by Dotty, and congratulated by a bunch of people (even though I noticed Marley didn't come around this time), there was one other thing I wanted to do while I still had the chance.

See, if you hadn't noticed, Miller gets in a good mood about once a century. I figured that if I ever wanted to ask him a favor, now was the time. So I told Mom I'd meet her in the parking lot, and then I went to look for him.

I know—kind of like looking for a speeding bus to walk in front of. But this was important.

When I found him, he was standing behind the snack bar, which was good. It gave me a tiny bit of privacy to ask him what I wanted to ask.

"Hey, Miller?" I said.

"*What?*" he said.

When he looked me in the eye, I lost a little of my nerve. But I couldn't stop now.

"You know our little deal, right?" I asked.

"Yeah. You score, you get to live," Miller said.

"Right," I said, "Well, I was thinking—"

"I'm bored already. Hurry up," he said.

"Let's say I score again next game," I said. "How about if you start leaving Maya, Jonny, and Dee-Dee alone too? Not just me."

Miller laughed right in my face, like he actually thought that was funny.

"What are you trying to do, renegotiate your contract? This isn't the NFL, Khatchadorkian," he said.

"I know," I said, "but—"

"I have a deal with *you*. Not every loser in this school," Miller said. "And the only reason I'm being so nice is 'cause I want to win games."

"Will you just think about it?" I said. "Please?"

"Yeah, I'll think about it," he said.

"Thanks," I told him.

"I'm done thinking," he said. "Now get out of here. I've gotta whizz."

"On the snack bar?" I said.

"GO!" Miller said, in that voice that usually comes right before something more painful.

But then the back door of the snack bar opened, and Jeanne was standing there, holding a bag of garbage.

"Oh!" she said. "Hi, Miller. Hi, Rafe."

"Hey, Jeanne," I said. I could tell she hadn't seen the game because she didn't say anything about it.

"Can one of you guys you do me a favor and put this in the Dumpster?" she asked, and held out the garbage.

"Um..." I said.

"Rafe can do it," Miller said. "He was just leaving. Weren't you, Khatchadorian?"

So much for asking favors.

"Yeah," I said. "I guess I was."

Or impressing Jeanne, for that matter.

Because that's what football heroes do after the game, right? They take out the garbage.

CHAPTER 59

IN THE NEWS

When I got to school the next day, I was still thinking about that football game. But all of that changed when I saw the Channel 11 news van parked out front.

It was sitting right there when I got off the bus. Some guy with a microphone and a cameraman was talking to the kids who were getting dropped off by their parents.

In fact, he was talking to Jeanne and her mom when I walked by.

"I *do* think it's a good thing," Jeanne was saying. "Everyone knows bullying is a problem, but nobody ever does anything about it."

Well, you *know* that got my attention. Time to pull my trusty old stalling trick. I stopped right there on the sidewalk and started tying my shoe, really slowly.

"So why do you think bullying is such a big problem at Hills Village Middle School?" the reporter guy asked her.

"I think it's a problem everywhere," Jeanne said. "And if something like this gets people talking, then I'm all for it. It's a pretty clear message, right? Just—be nice."

I almost said "YEAH!" right out loud, but I covered it up with a cough at the last second. Then my fake cough turned into a real one, and I started hacking so much that Jeanne and the reporter guy turned around to look at me.

That's when I got the heck out of there. The last thing I needed right now was a camera in my face.

Still, I was pretty excited. I couldn't believe someone would want to do a real news story about *my* art project. (Correction: an anonymous art project that just happened to be done by me.) I guess a bunch of kids must have gone home talking about it the day before, and one thing must have led to another.

Not that I was complaining or anything. Because it looked like SAM was hitting the big time. How crazy was *that*?

(Hint: not as crazy as it was going to get before it was all over. In fact, just keep reading.)

CHAPTER 60

SPECIAL SESSION

That day in Learning Skills, Mr. Fanucci had a "special session" for us Specials. He started off talking about the BNICE thing and what it all meant, and asking us what we thought about it.

Which basically meant I was keeping a *much* bigger secret than I ever thought I'd have to keep. My head felt like one of those vinegar-and-baking-soda volcanoes, just about ready to spew.

"I've been thinking about it," Mr. Fanucci said, "and I know you guys aren't crazy about meeting here in the fishbowl..."

That's what everyone called it—the fishbowl, since the whole world could see us sitting in there.

"...so I found a different space for Learning Skills."

That got a round of applause from Flip, Maya, Dee-Dee, and Jonny. I think I clapped a few times, but I was mostly watching the computers in the library. That's where everyone was still checking out my stuff—including Miller and Tug, sitting in their usual spots.

"But I also want you guys to let me know if anyone's giving you a hard time," Mr. F kept going. "And I want you to look out for one another too. Is that fair?"

"You bet, Mr. F," Flip said. "Don't worry. We will."

Remember when Miller gave Factoid a hard time and I didn't look out for him? Unfortunately, so do I. So I kept my eyes on the window into the library.

Tug had just clicked onto the home page for Art-Gunk.com, and Miller was staring at this one

BNICE picture like he was trying to figure out if it was *him* behind that red silhouette.

It was.

"What about you, Rafe?" Mr. Fanucci said. "Do you want to say anything about this BNICE business? Or bullying here at school?"

I looked over at Mr. F. "Not really," I said.

"Come on, Rafe," he said. "Let's have some participation. This is about you too, you know."

"Believe me, I know," I said. He didn't have any clue how funny that was, but I wasn't about to tell him.

"I want you to pay attention to what's going on," Mr. Fanucci said.

"I am," I said. And I was. Just not in the way he thought. "I, uh…I think it's great we're going to change classrooms."

"Well, I'm glad you're glad, anyway," he said. He was still staring at me, but as soon as he looked away, I looked back out at the library again.

And that's when everything went straight to Code Red.

Because, with my rotten luck, Tug had found another page on Art-Gunk. A very familiar page. One that I'd created myself.

That's right. He'd found my Loozer comics. The ones by *R. K.* (as in Rafe Khatchadorian) Whatchamacallit. The ones with the main character who looked waaaaay too much like me for comfort.

The ones on the very same website as the BNICE pics, starring Miller himself. He might be a red blob, but everyone knew it was him.

So imagine this next part in slow motion, because that's how it felt.

Tug stared at those comics.

Tug tapped Miller on the shoulder and said something to him.

Miller looked at Tug's computer.

Miller looked at his own computer.

Then back at Tug's computer.

Tug said something else.

And then...super...slowly...Miller turned around and looked at me through that fishbowl glass. The corners of his mouth went south, his eyes turned all red and homicidal, and his whole expression looked like one big flashing sign.

And the sign read, WELCOME BACK TO MILLER THE KILLERVILLE.

CHAPTER 61

MiNe

As soon as the bell rang for the end of class, I started looking for a safe exit.

I looked at the ceiling tiles. Any way of leaving straight up? Nope. And I definitely couldn't dig my way out. In fact, there was only one way to leave the fishbowl, and that was through the library.

So I tried to make it quick and kept my eyes down. Like that was ever going to work.

Miller slid his chair right in my way—with him in it, of course.

"What's up, Khatchadorkian?" he said.

"Nothing," I said. Mostly I was wondering— if Miller killed me right now, but he did it really quietly, would Mrs. Seagrave even care?

The first thing he did was tap his pencil on Tug's computer, with my Loozer comic sitting there on the screen.

"I always knew you were a loser," he said. "I just didn't know you'd made it official."

There wasn't any time to come up with a plan, so I went with my old standby: deny, deny, deny, deny, deny.

"I don't know what you mean," I told him.

"I *mean*..." Miller pointed back at his own computer, with that BNICE picture on it. "It looks to me like you've been busy. And I don't remember giving any permission to have someone spying on me and taking pictures."

I felt like a tree that had been chopped down and hadn't fallen over yet. But Miller would be fixing that real soon, thanks to his gigantic fists.

But then I heard someone behind me. It was Flip.

"Actually, Miller, those are *my* pictures," he said. "I took them."

"Huh?" I said. I turned around and Flip was holding up his phone.

"See?" he said.

"Hang on a second," Miller said. But then—

"No, they're mine," Maya said. She was standing behind Flip, along with Jonny and Dee-Dee.

"Yeah, right!" Tug said.

"Wrong again. They're my pictures," Dee-Dee said. "I did them on my iPad."

"Obviously those were all done by me," Jonny said. "Anyone can see that."

Miller looked at Tug, and Tug looked at Miller. Then both of them looked from me to Flip, to Maya, to Dee-Dee, and to Jonny. You could have heard a tumbleweed blow through that library just then.

So while Miller was still picking his jaw up off the ground, we all booked out of there. I knew I wasn't out of the woods yet, but it bought me a little time, anyway.

"Wow," I said, once we were in the hall. "Thanks, you guys." I couldn't believe what had just happened.

Except, I could too.

"That was awesome!" Flip said.

"Miller's still going to be mad," I said. "*Really* mad."

"Don't sweat it," he told me, but Flip never worries about anything. "Come on, you guys. Let's go eat lunch. Chocolate milk's on Rafe!"

They all headed for the cafeteria, but I hung back. I'd just figured out that I had another stop to make.

"You guys go ahead," I said, and I gave Flip some money out of my pocket. "Get started without me."

"Save you a seat?" Maya said.

"Um…I'm not sure," I told them.

Because where I was going now, it was hard to say when I'd be coming back.

BiG MeSS

As soon as I left the library, I went straight to the principal's office. I think it's the first time in the history of me getting in trouble that I actually sent *myself* there.

I figured this was the only chance I had to make things better. Not great, but better, anyway.

I told Mrs. Stricker everything. I told her I was SAM. I told her it was my fault that Channel 11 had shown up, even though I wasn't the one who called them. I even told her I was sorry, which I was. Sort of.

She didn't exactly die of shock. But she told me to expect a conference with Mom. And if you've been following my story at all, then you know that nothing good ever happens during those conferences.

By the end of the school day, Mom was already there. She looked like she was in one of those movies where the person keeps waking up and having the same day, over and over.

I kind of felt the same way.

For a little while, Mom and Mrs. Stricker talked by themselves. Then they pulled me in there, and I got my punishment: *eight detentions*. That was one for every picture I'd taken and posted without people's permission. (Good thing they didn't know about the ninety-five pictures I *didn't* use!) I also had to take them all down from the site and write a report about privacy.

But that wasn't the really bad part. Or at least, not the worst part.

Mom told me to get my stuff, and that we were going to go home and have a talk. So I walked up the hall to my locker, and when I went past the library, I saw some after-school kids hanging out at the computers. But they weren't looking at my SAM stuff this time. They were looking at Loozer. I guess word was already spreading that the mystery was solved, and that I was SAM, and that I was also a big fat you-know-what.

When I got to my locker, I saw that someone—maybe Miller, maybe not—had left a little art of their own.

That was the worst part. Or at least, that was the beginning of it.

WHAT DO YOU SAY?

When we got home, Mom sat me down at the kitchen table and took a deep breath.

"Explain," she said. That was it.

I didn't know what she was looking for, or what kind of explanation I was supposed to give. So I just started with the thing I was thinking about the most. That's when I showed her my Loozer comics.

And get this. She actually liked them. She even laughed a couple times and told me that they were good but also that she had some questions.

"I thought Leo was a secret for you," she said. "I didn't realize you had started telling people about him."

"He is! And I didn't!" I said. "I mean—I didn't mean to. I just figured nobody at HVMS would ever see those comics. In fact, I didn't think anyone would notice them at all."

"Well, that's a lesson," Mom said. "I'm sorry, Rafe, but it is. Posting your comics online means you lose all control of what happens to them. That's not always a bad thing. People get to see your art that way. But you need to think about what it means to make it available like that."

I knew, I knew, I knew.

Or at least, I did now.

"I have another question," Mom said. "What made you want to include Leo in the first place?"

"Well..." I said. "I don't know if this is going to sound weird, but it was like he wanted to be in there. He kind of asked."

"I can understand that," Mom said.

Mom's used to the way I talk to Leo sometimes. But she also seemed a little sad. Not about me. About Leo. After all, he was her son the way he was also my brother. And then he died. It's not exactly the happiest subject in our house, even though we all still love him.

"What do I do now?" I said. "I mean, what if people start asking me about him?"

"You tell them as much or as little as you want," Mom said. "It's up to you, Rafe. You can also just say, 'I don't want to talk about any of that.' Period."

"Yeah," I said. I knew she was right, but it still felt complicated. Leo had been a secret for a long time. And even though I was the one who put him in the comic, I didn't know what I was supposed to do about it now.

"One more question," Mom said. "I want to ask you about this Loozer character."

Oh, man. Here it was.

"Do you feel like a loser?" she said. "Is that where these comics are coming from?"

I knew that was what she was going to ask. But still, when I started to answer, it was like my throat got shut down for repairs. I felt like I had two pieces of double-stick tape down there, with a golf ball stuck in the middle.

Finally, I just said, "I don't want to talk about any of that."

"Period?" Mom said, with this nice smile.

I just nodded, 'cause I was afraid that golf ball was going to turn into a crying thing if I said anything else.

"Fair enough," she said. Then she grabbed me and gave me this big hug instead of lecturing me or talking any more.

And you know what? I cried anyway. It wasn't a big deal. I've cried in front of Mom before. Heck, I've cried in front of *you* before, if you've read some of my other stories. I guess I just had to "get it out." That's what Mom calls it.

So I did.

Lucky for me, Georgia was at a friend's house, so I didn't have to explain anything to her nosy face. But Junior was right there. He put his chin on my leg and I patted him on the head, which made me feel better too. For real. He's a great dog. And even if I felt crappy just then, I knew it was going to be okay. Maybe not in five minutes. Or even five days. But soon, anyway.

For starters, Mom was way less mad about Operation: S.A.M. than I thought. She said putting up my pictures of famous paintings hadn't done any harm, and I think she was even a little proud of my idea. She didn't give me any punishment on top of those detentions. In fact, she didn't even make me quit football.

And that brings me right up to the next thing in this crazy story.

Which also happens to be my favorite part.

CHAPTER 64

END RUN

Flash forward! Again!

It was game three of the Falcons' season. We were playing the Sloatsburg Middle School Rams, and the score was 7–7, coming down to the end of the fourth quarter.

We knew we had to score soon if we were going to have any chance of winning. There was enough time for one turnaround, but that would just put the ball in Sloatsburg's hands. It was all down to this.

"All right, let's do it," Coach said. "Highway Eleven, guys. Highway Eleven."

We didn't have a lot of audibles for plays, but everyone knew this one by now. We'd practiced it all week. Highway Eleven was the name for my special take-the-hand-off-and-run play.

Quinn had scored our first touchdown of the game, so nobody from Sloatsburg had even seen Highway Eleven yet. Which made it our secret weapon. Which kind of made *me* our secret weapon.

And that's when I got my next, brand-new, really big, really good idea—right there, walking onto the field for the play. I never even saw it coming until the idea hit me all at once, like a strike of lightning to the brain.

Miller never saw it coming either.

"Hey, Miller," I said. "You know that deal I asked you about before?"

"Huh?" he said.

I slowed down and kept my voice low. "You know. About Maya, Jonny, and Dee-Dee?"

"Not now," Miller said.

"Yes. Now," I said.

Then I stopped, knelt down, and started tying my shoe. Even though it didn't need tying.

"What are you doing?" Miller said. "Get up."

I kept my face down so only he could hear. "I score, and you leave my friends alone," I told him.

"Let's go, Khatchadorian!" Coach yelled. "Keep it moving."

"Yeah, Khatchadorian," Miller said, squinting at me like he had fists for eyeballs. "Keep it moving."

"Do we have a deal?" I asked him. "Or do I get lost on the way to the end zone?"

My heart was banging around playing defensive tackle against my ribs, but I held my ground.

"Here's your deal," Miller said. "Run the play or die."

"All *riiiight*," I said, making it sound a lot like *You'll be sorrrry*.

He didn't even answer. But I could tell I had him feeling kind of nervous now. He wanted to win this game. Miller wanted to win *every* game, which was a definite advantage for me.

"You sure about this?" I said while we were still getting into position.

"Shut up, you guys," Jeremy said. The ref handed Quinn the ball, and we all got ready for the snap.

"Hike…" Tug called.

"Positive?" I said, so Miller could hear me.

"Shut up!" Tug said.

"What?" Quinn said.

"Not you," Tug said.

"Last chance," I said to Miller.

"Hike…" Tug called, and even then, I was still looking at Miller like I was thinking, *Now, what am I supposed to do for this play again?* Miller stared back too. Right up until the very…last… millisecond.

"Okay, okay!" he yelled. "Deal!"

Quinn snapped the ball. Tug took it. Miller started blocking. I left him behind, turned around, grabbed that hand-off from Tug, and ran like it was what I'd been put on this planet to do. For real.

All the guys opened up a lane for me, and ten seconds later, I was down there at the far end of Highway Eleven—right inside the end zone.

Touchdown!

Final score, 13–7.

Hills Village goes 2–1 for the season so far.

And I'd just renegotiated my contract with Miller.

CHAPTER 65

GOOD (FOR NOW)

I know what you're thinking. Miller's not exactly dependable. All he had to do was say "deal" and then turn around and break his word. It wouldn't be the first lie he ever told. Or the thousandth.

But here's something that maybe you don't know. I was never going to blow that play. No way. I like scoring touchdowns the way I like to eat—as much and as often as possible. Maybe I'm not the world's most "well-rounded" player, but at least I've got quick feet and Highway Eleven going for me.

I just had to out-bluff Miller one time. And that's what I did. Now we have the weirdest truce in the history of truces. As long as he thinks I'm willing to sacrifice a touchdown, or even a game, he'll play along just the way I asked him to.

And for the rest of football season, life's going to be a little bit easier for Jonny, Dee-Dee, Maya, and yes, me.

Did that make me finally like playing? Not necessarily, but it did make me like scoring!

After football season's over...well, I don't know what happens then. Maybe Miller and I will go from football season right back into hunting season. But I'll deal with that later. Meanwhile, I'm just taking it one thing at a time.

And most importantly, making my *own* choices.

And if you ask me, I'm doing pretty good at it too.

I GOTTA BE ME

So maybe that's not much, but it's way better than nothing.

Ms. Donatello says when you change one little corner of the world, you change the world. I don't know if that's true, but if it is, then I say mission accomplished.

My BNICE project ended up changing things too, in an even bigger way. I know that one news story on Channel 11 and a couple of conversations around school aren't going to drive bullies extinct everywhere, but they made a difference at HVMS.

Pretty soon after I confessed to Mrs. Stricker, she sent all the students home with a letter to our parents. It talked about bullying and how it wouldn't be tolerated at HVMS. (Except by her, obviously. Kidding. Kind of.) She was even going to start a task force with students, teachers, and parents to figure out how we can safely report bullying incidents—and hopefully stop them. It didn't mention BNICE, but everyone knew that was why she wrote the letter.

And if anything was going to help keep Miller off our backs, I was all for it.

And speaking of BNICE, Ms. D ended up giving me an A– for the assignment. She said that it was
"creatively rendered" and that I'd made a really worthwhile statement.

"That grade is for your art, *not* your methods," she said. "No more spying or taking pictures of people without their permission, okay?"

"I got it," I said. "Seriously."

I think she believed me too. Because then she let me in on a little secret of her own. As far as I know, I'm the only one she told. So if you see Mrs. Stricker around, keep your mouth shut about this, okay?

Here's something else. After people got tired of calling me Loozer and asking questions about Leo, I think they actually started liking my comics. I'm up to a hundred and twelve followers on Art-Gunk, which is about a hundred and ten more than I ever expected to have. (I knew Mom and Flip would get on board.)

That's not bad. I think once everyone at HVMS stopped laughing at me, they started laughing at Loozer and Leo instead. Which was the whole idea. I even told a few people about Leo being my brother. They don't need to know that I still talk to him sometimes, though. That part's mine. And Leo's too, of course.

So I'm going to keep doing those comics, but with my own name now. No more R. K. Whatchamacallit. And I retired SAM too. Once the whole fake identity thing is gone, there's not much "secret" left in the Secret Artist Man.

Which is okay. To tell you the truth, I don't think I want to be a secret artist man anymore. Just plain old *artist* sounds good to me.

SAM out.

CHAPTER 67

YOU DOG!

So there I was, walking Junior early that Sunday morning. We headed over to the dog park, like always, and it was practically deserted when we got there.

But guess who *was* there, throwing a rubber bone around and playing with her dog?

Marley Grote, that's who.

I was pretty sure Marley couldn't have cared less about me by then. I mean, it wasn't like she was going out of her way to talk to me anymore. Or even coming to the games. I almost turned around and headed home just then.

But Junior had other ideas. The second he saw Justine Bieber, he started barking like crazy and pulling my arm out of the socket with his leash.

So I opened the gate and let him off the leash. What else was I going to do?

"Hey, Marley," I said.

"Hi, Rafe," she said, kind of friendly and kind of not friendly at the same time. "How's it going?"

"So-so," I said. "A little weird, if you want to know the truth. But I understand if you don't want to talk to me."

"What do you mean?" she asked.

"I mean, the way you've been ignoring me ever since all that Loozer stuff," I said. "It's okay. I get it."

I figured there wasn't any reason to hide anymore. In fact, it made me a little mad when I thought about it.

But then Marley said, "I haven't been ignoring you. You've been ignoring *me*."

"Huh?" I said, and Marley rolled her eyes.

"I think I made it pretty obvious I liked you, Rafe. It was getting embarrassing, if you want to know the truth. Sorry, but I'm not that desperate," she said.

This was a whole new side of Marley I hadn't seen before. It was all like one big WOW in my brain.

"So I don't get it," I said. "Do you think I'm a total jerk, or not?"

"Not," she said. "I think what you did at school is pretty great."

"But you don't even come to the games anymore," I said.

"I'm not talking about football," she said. "I'm talking about all that 'Be Nice' stuff, and the way you stuck up for all the kids like us at HVMS."

"Like…us?" I said.

"Face it, Rafe. We're not exactly the most popular sandwiches at the picnic," Marley said.

The more this went on, the less I understood. It's not like Marley was in Learning Skills. She just seemed kind of normal to me. But maybe she didn't *feel* normal.

Which made me like her more.

And then she said, "So you noticed I don't come to the games anymore, huh?"

That was embarrassing, but I couldn't take it back now.

"Yeah," I said.

"Do you *want* me to come to the games?" she asked.

"Yeah," I said. "I think I do. I mean—yes. I do."

"Okay," she said. "I will."

Then Marley leaned right in and kissed me, right there in the park. And right on the lips too. It lasted for at least five seconds. I'm not even sure how long. But I kissed her back, if you want to know. I didn't even run away this time.

"Um, thanks," I said when it was over. I didn't know what else to say, or even think. My brain was like some kind of slot machine with those wheels spinning around, too fast to see anything.

"You're welcome," Marley said. Now she looked kind of embarrassed. And then *I* was kind of embarrassed. My face was hot, and hers was red, and everything seemed kind of weird for a second there.

But then we both looked over at our dogs. They were having a good time and sniffing each other's butts on the other side of the park—and something about that made us both crack up at the same time. Which was kind of perfect.

So that's it. I don't have any other "first kiss" stories to compare mine to, and I don't know if all of that is totally lame, or what. But maybe it doesn't even matter, because you know what else? This one's mine.

And I'll take it.

CHAPTER 68

LASAGNA, APPLE PIE, AND ICE CREAM

Speaking of embarrassing, here's a whole *other* nutso thing I have to tell you about.

You might have noticed Mom and Mr. Fanucci have been showing up in a lot of the same chapters all through this book. Believe me, *I* noticed.

So it wasn't a lot longer after all this stuff happened that Mr. Fanucci came over for dinner the first time. He even said I could call him Ed when he was at the house, but not in school. Which was all just *so weird*.

Maybe Mom likes him because my grades have started looking up. I think those Learning Skills classes are actually paying off, and that's all thanks to Mr. Fanucci...I mean, Ed...I mean, Mr. Fun. (Do you see what I mean? *Weird*.)

I don't really know where it all goes from here. But I guess that isn't so different from the rest of my life. I never know what's going to happen next. I'm not sure where the whole "me and Marley" thing is going either. Or the whole "Flip thinks Georgia is cute" thing. The only ones who totally make sense, if you ask me, are Junior and Justine Bieber.

Oh, and Grandma Dotty too. Sometimes she makes the most sense of all.

She also makes the best lasagna ever. It goes great with apple pie from Swifty's Diner and a giant scoop of vanilla ice cream. And in my book, there's not a whole lot better than that.

Happy football season, everyone! Catch you next time!

NOT-SO-MERRY CHRISTMAS

I slammed my sketchbook closed. Usually drawing comics made me feel better, but not today. It was Christmas morning, and even Loozer was having a better time than I was.

As for Leo, well…I can explain about him later.

I didn't exactly get a hoverboard and a ski trip under the tree that morning. Instead, I got some school clothes and two new books from Mom. Also a coupon from my sister, Georgia, for one turn unloading the dishwasher, and a "Christmas hug" from Grandma Dotty. Grandma said she was still working on her gifts.

The other thing I didn't get was a WormHole Premium Multi-Platform GameBox. That's what I *really* wanted, but I would have had a better chance asking Santa for the Empire State Building. Those WormHoles were *expensive*, and we weren't exactly rolling in dough that Christmas.

Still, I would have given my big toe for one of those systems. They could run games from all the other major brands, plus their own titles, which were the best ones out there, by far. That thing could practically clean your room and do your homework for you, it was *that* cool.

Not that I was obsessed or anything.

Well, okay, maybe a little bit.

But none of that was the *real* bummer.

"All right, I've got to get going," Mom said. It was only eleven in the morning, but she was putting on her coat to go to work. Yeah, that's right. On Christmas. The Madison Hotel was paying really good money for waitresses in their banquet hall that day, and Mom couldn't afford to say no.

"I'll make it up to you guys," she said. "I'm off all day tomorrow and we'll have a real Christmas dinner then."

What were we going to say? It's not like Mom

wanted to work on Christmas. She was just
looking out for us. The least we could do was act
like it was no big deal.

"That sounds awesome!" I said.

"It'll be like having two Christmases!"
Grandma said.

"Yeah!" Georgia said. "No problem, Mom."

I think she actually bought it too. And we might have pulled it off, if I hadn't opened my big mouth one more time. See, I have this bad habit of taking things a little too far sometimes.

Or a lot too far.

"Don't worry about it, Mom," I said. "Who needs Christmas, anyway? Not us!"

Yeah, right. Like any kid who celebrates Christmas was going to say *that*.

That's when Mom stopped buttoning her coat. She gave me this weird smile and her eyes got kind of watery.

"I'll be right back," she said. "I, um…forgot my keys."

Then she went into the bathroom and closed the door behind her. (FYI, Mom doesn't keep her keys in the bathroom.) She'd been spending a lot of time in there ever since she and my Learning Skills teacher, Mr. Fanucci, decided to stop dating after a while. I'll admit it kind of skeeved me out that they were seeing each other, but I'd one thousand times rather see them kissing than to see my mom sad.

"Way to go, big mouth," Georgia said.

"But…" I said. "I didn't mean to—"

"Yeah, you never do, Rafe," she said. Even Grandma was looking at me like I'd just taken the world's cruddiest Christmas and managed to make it even cruddier.

Which I guess I had.

Leave it to me.

So basically, that was strike one. I'll tell you about strike two in a minute. But the point is, my little Christmas disaster was the beginning of everything else that happened that winter.

I'm talking about how I got in hot water with Mom, almost lost my best friend (the furry one), launched my very own business empire, survived the Great Dog War of January, and learned a little magic along the way.

Which may not be where you thought this was going, but it totally is.

Read on, my friend.

THE MIDDLE SCHOOL SERIES

THE WORST YEARS OF MY LIFE
(with Chris Tebbetts)

This is the insane story of my first year at middle school, when I, Rafe Khatchadorian, took on a real-life bear (sort of), sold my soul to the school bully, and fell for the most popular girl in school. Come join me, if you dare…

GET ME OUT OF HERE!
(with Chris Tebbetts)

We've moved to the big city, where I'm going to a super-fancy art school. The first project is to create something based on our exciting lives. But my life is TOTALLY BORING. It's time for Operation Get a Life.

MY BROTHER IS A BIG, FAT LIAR
(with Lisa Papademetriou)

So you've heard all about my big brother, Rafe, and now it's time to set the record straight. (Almost) EVERYTHING he says is a Big, Fat Lie. I'm Georgia, and it's time for some payback…Khatchadorian style.

HOW I SURVIVED BULLIES, BROCCOLI, AND SNAKE HILL
(with Chris Tebbetts)

I'm excited for a fun summer at camp—until I find out it's a summer *school* camp. There's no fun and games here, just a whole lotta trouble!

ULTIMATE SHOWDOWN
(with Julia Bergen)

Who would have thought that we—Rafe and Georgia—would ever agree on anything? That's right—we're writing a book together. And the best part? We want you to be part of the fun too!

SAVE RAFE!
(with Chris Tebbetts)

I'm in worse trouble than ever! I need to survive a gut-bustingly impossible outdoor excursion so I can return to school next year. But will I get through in one piece?

JUST MY ROTTEN LUCK
(with Chris Tebbetts)

I'm heading back to Hills Village Middle School, but only if I take "special" classes... If that wasn't bad enough, when I somehow land a place on the school football team, I find myself playing alongside the biggest bully in school, Miller the Killer!

DOG'S BEST FRIEND
(with Chris Tebbetts)
It's a dog-eat-dog world. When I start my own dog-walking empire, I didn't think it could go so horribly wrong! Somehow, I always seem to end up in deep doo-doo…

ESCAPE TO AUSTRALIA
(with Martin Chatterton)
I just won an all-expenses paid trip of a lifetime to Australia. But here's the bad news: I MIGHT NOT MAKE IT OUT ALIVE!

FROM HERO TO ZERO
(with Chris Tebbetts)
I'm going on the class trip of a lifetime! What could possibly go wrong? I've spent all of middle school being chased by Miller the Killer, but on this trip, there's NOWHERE TO RUN!

BORN TO ROCK
(with Chris Tebbetts)
My brother, Rafe Khatchadorian, has been public enemy #1 my whole life. But if I want to win the Battle of the Bands, I'm going to have to recruit the most devious person I know…

FIELD TRIP FIASCO
(with Martin Chatterton)
GUESS WHERE I'M GOING? ON AN ALL-EXPENSES-PAID ART TRIP TO CALIFORNIA! And this time, nothing's going to go wrong! Famous last words, right?

ALSO BY JAMES PATTERSON

MIDDLE SCHOOL SERIES
The Worst Years of My Life (*with Chris Tebbetts*)
Get Me Out of Here! (*with Chris Tebbetts*)
My Brother Is a Big, Fat Liar (*with Lisa Papademetriou*)
How I Survived Bullies, Broccoli, and Snake Hill
(*with Chris Tebbetts*)
Ultimate Showdown (*with Julia Bergen*)
Save Rafe! (*with Chris Tebbetts*)
Just My Rotten Luck (*with Chris Tebbetts*)
Dog's Best Friend (*with Chris Tebbetts*)
Escape to Australia (*with Martin Chatterton*)
From Hero to Zero (*with Chris Tebbetts*)
Born to Rock (*with Chris Tebbetts*)
Master of Disaster (*with Chris Tebbetts*)
Field Trip Fiasco (*with Chris Tebbetts*)

DOG DIARIES SERIES
Dog Diaries (*with Steven Butler*)
Happy Howlidays! (*with Steven Butler*)
Mission Impawsible (*with Steven Butler*)
Curse of the Mystery Mutt (*with Steven Butler*)
Camping Chaos! (*with Steven Butler*)
Dinosaur Disaster! (*with Steven Butler*)
Big Top Bonanza! (*with Steven Butler*)

THE I FUNNY SERIES
I Funny (*with Chris Grabenstein*)
I Even Funnier (*with Chris Grabenstein*)
I Totally Funniest (*with Chris Grabenstein*)
I Funny TV (*with Chris Grabenstein*)
School of Laughs (*with Chris Grabenstein*)
The Nerdiest, Wimpiest, Dorkiest I Funny Ever
(*with Chris Grabenstein*)

MAX EINSTEIN SERIES
The Genius Experiment (*with Chris Grabenstein*)
Rebels with a Cause (*with Chris Grabenstein*)
Saves the Future (*with Chris Grabenstein*)
World Champions! (*with Chris Grabenstein*)

TREASURE HUNTERS SERIES
Treasure Hunters (*with Chris Grabenstein*)
Danger Down the Nile (*with Chris Grabenstein*)
Secret of the Forbidden City (*with Chris Grabenstein*)
Peril at the Top of the World (*with Chris Grabenstein*)
Quest for the City of Gold (*with Chris Grabenstein*)
All-American Adventure (*with Chris Grabenstein*)
The Plunder Down Under (*with Chris Grabenstein*)

HOUSE OF ROBOTS SERIES
House of Robots (*with Chris Grabenstein*)
Robots Go Wild! (*with Chris Grabenstein*)
Robot Revolution (*with Chris Grabenstein*)

JACKY HA-HA SERIES
Jacky Ha-Ha (*with Chris Grabenstein*)
My Life is a Joke (*with Chris Grabenstein*)

OTHER ILLUSTRATED NOVELS
Kenny Wright: Superhero (*with Chris Tebbetts*)
Homeroom Diaries (*with Lisa Papademetriou*)
Word of Mouse (*with Chris Grabenstein*)
Pottymouth and Stoopid (*with Chris Grabenstein*)
Laugh Out Loud (*with Chris Grabenstein*)
Not So Normal Norbert (*with Joey Green*)
Unbelievably Boring Bart (*with Duane Swierczynski*)
Katt vs. Dogg (*with Chris Grabenstein*)
Katt Loves Dogg (*with Chris Grabenstein*)

For more information about James Patterson's novels,
visit www.penguin.co.uk